DRAGON REVEALED

DRAGON REVEALED
DRAGON APPARENT™ BOOK THREE

TALIA BECKETT

This book is a work of fiction. All of the characters, organizations, and events portrayed in this novel are either products of the author's imagination or are used fictitiously. Sometimes both.

Copyright © 2022 Talia Beckett
Cover by Bandrei
Cover copyright © LMBPN Publishing

LMBPN Publishing supports the right to free expression and the value of copyright. The purpose of copyright is to encourage writers and artists to produce the creative works that enrich our culture.

The distribution of this book without permission is a theft of the author's intellectual property. If you would like permission to use material from the book (other than for review purposes), please contact support@lmbpn.com. Thank you for your support of the author's rights.

LMBPN Publishing
PMB 196, 2540 South Maryland Pkwy
Las Vegas, NV 89109

Version 1.00 December, 2022
eBook ISBN: 979-8-88541-778-5
Print ISBN: 979-8-88878-029-9

THE DRAGON REVEALED TEAM

Thanks to the JIT Team:

Christopher Gilliard
Dorothy Lloyd
Jeff Goode
Paul Westman
Jan Hunnicutt
Zacc Pelter

To Bryan. I am loving doing life with you by my side. You're my favorite person to adventure and do life with. I had no idea that we could have so much fun and tackling life's problems could feel so simple.

— Talia

CHAPTER ONE

As I stepped into yet another classroom in yet another tower, I fought to keep my cool. Today was one of those days where I was more than ready to smack someone. Neritas was by my side, and Flick wasn't far behind. My skill level had finally gotten me bumped up to classes with other dragons of a similar age.

That part was a relief. I was more than over having lessons with dragons a lot younger than me. I'd had to do that at first because I'd spent most of my life not knowing that I was a dragon. Thankfully, other than some dull history lessons, I was now upgraded across the board. On some subjects, I was actually ahead and had human-equivalent exam results to prove it.

I still didn't like all of my lessons, however. And Practical Magic was one of those lessons I didn't like much.

Now and then, I learned something new. But I'd fought shadow catchers and used my abilities in combat to escape from them on numerous occasions. I was already more experienced than everyone else in the class, and I suspected that included my teacher. Until I'd proved this beyond all reasonable doubt, I had to endure the lessons, however.

And endure them I did. I barely had to concentrate as I made different things light up and others darken, including my own body. At the same time, I kept up a conversation with Neritas and Flick about their gifts and tried to discover what else they could do. It wasn't easy to practice as much as I thought we ought to, given what was out in the world, but Flick could make all sorts of things crackle with electricity, and that was entertaining, if nothing else.

Neritas was on the other side of me, almost refusing to do anything.

One of the other dragons came closer, tensing up with effort until he managed to light up a light bulb and grinning at his success.

"Look, Red, I can do the same thing as you. What's so amazing about your color?"

I wasn't sure what to do at first, all of me wanting to smack him one or make his light bulb glow so bright that it blinded him and everyone around him, but Neritas put a hand on my shoulder.

As I glanced his way, he subtly shook his head. I turned my back on him and walked back to stand beside Flick. I watched him smirk and also hold up the light bulb he'd been given. It was glowing even brighter, but it was shaded more pink than the other.

"You have to admit—tech has made at least some of what you can do possible."

"It has. And I don't mind that. I don't see the point in wasting my energy on lighting shit up that doesn't need it."

"So you mean we can do that for you, your highness?" Flick asked, his grin growing wider. I knew he was teasing me, and he'd said it quietly enough that I knew only Neritas heard it, as Flick had intended.

In response, I looked at the other three light bulbs on the table and made them all glow, though they weren't connected to me.

"Show-off," he muttered and let his light bulb fizzle out.

"What does it feel like knowing technology can outdo your power?" one of the female dragons suddenly asked, walking up closer, with several other dragons taking an interest and coming up closer too. "You're the last red dragon left, aren't you? And there's no use for you in the world anymore."

"Please, can we all focus on our tasks and learning how to use our own powers," the teacher said, but the other dragons ignored him, loads of the yellow dragons holding light bulbs and coming closer.

"Sir, we're just trying to understand what the point of a red dragon is now. I mean, they're nothing special, and now that we don't have them on a throne anymore, they're useless as a species. So what's the point of Scarlet? Surely she's just a waste of space."

As soon as she finished speaking, I created a large well of darkness so pitch black and so large that it plunged the entire class into blackness. At the same time, I shrouded every single light bulb, including those that had been lit by electricity.

There were squeals all around, and I heard the crackles of electricity while all the yellow dragons tried to make their light bulbs work. Over my shoulder, Flick chuckled.

Again, I felt Neritas reach out and place his hand on my shoulder.

Slowly, without saying a word, I let the darkness go, letting it get lighter and allowing the yellow dragons to work their light bulbs again until everything was back to normal.

I caught the smirk on the teacher's face too. He was getting an idea of exactly what I was capable of and clearly knew that I was far from a waste of space.

The dragons all looked at each other, none of them saying anything. I deliberately turned my back on them again and went back to controlling the smaller objects we were meant to practice with. I heard some of them muttering, but none of them spoke to me anymore, and Neritas took his hand off my shoulder.

It was only when he did that I realized I had been connected to him and his source of power. I didn't think I had drawn on it, and if I had left any mark or impression on him, he didn't show it. And I was sure we hadn't connected physically until after I'd made it dark.

Trying not to let my fear show, I straightened up and focused on the lesson again. There wasn't a lot for me to do, and I didn't need to prove anything to anyone regarding my powers and control ever again, but I wanted to look busy so the other dragons would leave me alone.

As if trying to help, Neritas handed me his shield, his long leather jacket fluttering in a slight breeze along the way. I grinned at the aesthetic. He had this bad boy look perfected, but he was less of a bad boy and more like someone who didn't want to fit in with a crowd he didn't like.

I was constantly thankful for Neritas and Flick. They were two very different dragons, and, in theory, they shouldn't have gotten along with each other. They had bonded over their mutual desire to protect me, though, and that kept them busy enough and on their toes enough that they didn't have a chance to focus on any differences.

Of course, I'd rather I didn't need them, but I didn't have much of a say in my day-to-day schedule, something that was strange to a person who, until a few weeks ago, was the complete ruler of her life, and in the dragon world was probably the heir to the throne.

I practiced lighting up the shield and making it dark, aware that I still had an awful lot of people looking at me. Wanting to try something that actually challenged me, I focused on lighting up only specific areas of the object while at the same time darkening other areas.

It didn't take long for me to figure out how to do that, either. I divided the shield up into halves, then quarters, and finally eighths. Once I'd done that without much of a struggle, I decided to make it all dark and then draw over its surface with a thin line of light. It wasn't long before the dragons around me were all watching.

Art wasn't my strong suit, so the design was crude, but it showed off how well I could control the power I had. The parts of the shield I made dark were hard to look at, so dark it seemed to draw the eyesight in and make your vision go funny, and the lines were so bright you could look away and still see the pattern for a few seconds.

The classroom grew quieter until the only sounds I could hear were the beat of my own heart and the occasional exclamation as I made the pattern more intricate and kept going.

I lost track of time while I focused on pushing my ability to the limits and holding it in place. Eventually, our teacher placed his hand on my shoulder, my pattern at a good stopping point.

"I wish I could freeze this moment in time and share it with the entire city, but I don't doubt your classmates will tell of it themselves. I wish to see how far you can go, but we're already ten minutes over our class time, and I have to admit new students now."

"Sorry." I let the shield and the light return to normal.

A few of my classmates sighed when the shield went dark and became ordinary and plain again. I handed it back to the nearest black dragon and exhaled. After pushing my abilities so hard and concentrating for so long, I had a headache and didn't know if I could have done much more anyway.

I got a few nods of appreciation from classmates who had previously been cold toward me as everyone filed out, many of them more ready to leave than I was. It didn't take me long to gather up my tablet, rucksack, and the lesson notes I'd made by hand, but the rest of the class was gone by the time I was ready to leave.

Flick and Neritas fell in on either side of me and once again escorted me from the school room and to the next lesson I had with them. We had so many classes together now and ate together so often that I felt like we were hardly ever apart.

Our next lesson was a flying lesson. I had recently been promoted to join them. I wasn't as good yet, but I was getting closer. Jared, the flying instructor, had said I *would* soon be as good if I attended half my lessons with them and continued the other half by myself.

It also took some of the pressure off my companions.

Despite my love of flying, this was one of the lessons that always had me a little worried. Not about the actual flying and what I might be asked to do in that regard, but the animosity other dragons still held toward me could be dangerous when trying new maneuvers.

There was a strange new vibe to the class this time, however. Jared was deep in conversation with a couple of the students, and they all glanced my way a couple of times.

Again, some of my classmates smiled at me and appeared to be a little warmer generally. Maybe my display with the shield had done some good in addition to giving me the opportunity to practice.

Normally, my classmates made it difficult for me to get to the flying platform. Neritas and Flick had to force their way through with me between them, and Jared would encourage the others to let me come to the front. Today, however, they shuffled back a little and allowed us to take up places on the platform to wait our turn.

It didn't take long for Jared to stop talking. As soon as he did, he looked my way, met my gaze, and nodded as if he had heard about what I'd done and respected it too.

Feeling put on the spot and wishing everything would go back to normal, I tried not to meet the gaze of anyone else and hoped Jared would begin.

"We're a little late starting today, but I want to try and do the lesson I had planned, even if we run over as well."

A few people groaned and shot me dirty looks, clearly thinking I was to blame for lessons running over.

It wasn't going to help my standing with the other students that they now felt they had to suffer extra lesson time because of me. Some of them loved to fly, as I did, but I got the feeling the animosity from the others would outweigh the gain.

Thankfully, the lesson seemed to go by without any issues. No one tried to kill me while I flew. Or injure me. And that was my day done for a while.

"Want to go get some surf in before dinner?" Flick asked.

I considered the offer and how I felt about being on the beach. I hadn't gone there since shadow catchers had chased me from the nearby cave and into the water. While I knew that I was likely to be safe, I hadn't been out of the city in any way since defeating several of the creatures.

Eventually, I shook my head and declined the offer. I couldn't bring myself to head out of the city yet. After making excuses that weren't entirely a lie about being tired from my lessons, Flick and Neritas escorted me back to Ben's apartment.

I found the dragon sitting at his desk, where he normally did. He wasn't working on translating the journal. Instead, he was holding a pen and focusing on a sheet of paper. He stayed that way until I'd said goodbye to my friends and shut the door.

Certain that Ben must have found out something important, I hurried to him and plonked myself down. Only then did he look at me.

"What?" I asked when he didn't speak but studied my face instead.

"I hear that you made a bit of a display this afternoon." He took his time over his words.

"There was a moment where I tested my limits a little."

"A little?"

"I admit that I might have had a few more...witnesses than usual while I practiced. Most of the time, the class likes to ignore me, and this time they didn't. They challenged me, and I simply reacted."

Ben didn't respond, but a frown appeared on his face. This wasn't the reaction I'd have expected, but it also made me wonder how he knew so soon. It had only been a couple of hours at most.

Eventually, Ben sat back and threw his hands up in the air.

"Well, it's got you out of that particular lesson. Your tutor decided that you knew more than he could ever teach you already. You won't have to go back."

It was my turn to be silent, unable to reply. Of all the outcomes I had expected, that wasn't it. And I had no idea if it was a good thing or bad. Only time would tell.

CHAPTER TWO

As I finished eating, I pushed my knife and fork together and sat back. I'd made me and Ben dinner, and we'd talked about all sorts of small subjects while avoiding all the big ones. Although he hadn't said anything else about the lessons and me getting out of them in the future, I knew it weighed on his mind.

In truth, it was also still bothering me. There were a thousand different ways that everyone else could react to me not being taught Practical Magic anymore, and I also had the elders to worry about. We had been under so much scrutiny already, and I didn't want to invite any more. And it was all because I had decided to let my powers loose for once and try to see what I was capable of.

"What are you doing this evening?" I asked when Ben finished and sat back to study me.

Holding my shoulders back and trying to draw myself up to a more impressive height, I tried to look interested in the answer, a task that wasn't easy when I could only think about how difficult life was in the city and how a part of me wanted to go back to my apartment and Anthony. The dragon city still wasn't quite my home.

"I'm doing something that needs to be done. As I think I do all the time."

I raised my eyebrows, surprised by the sass and the frustration in his voice.

"You're angry?" I asked, trying to be diplomatic and find out what had bothered him before I got defensive or angry too. For a hotheaded red dragon, I thought it was progress.

This question seemed to make Ben exhale and deflate a little.

"Not angry, I guess. Just...frustrated that we have to be more careful than someone your age ought to be. That there's this pressure on you when, for a dragon, you're still incredibly young. That I'm not Anthony, and this isn't what he wanted for you. That your own parents can't be here to teach you what you really need to know. And that we still don't know for sure who they were, even though that knowledge could lead to more than one dragon wanting you dead."

"If they don't already want me dead anyway," I replied, trying to be glib and grin, but it fell flat. Though I'd been joking about being an annoying show-off, the statement held enough truth that the dark humor hadn't had the intended effect.

"Sorry," I added as I sat.

"It's not really your fault. You're navigating this as best you can. All things considered, you've done a good job so far. But we need to be careful. There's a fine balance between you defending yourself and drawing attention to yourself."

"And I crossed it today."

"I wish the answer to that question wasn't yes." Ben exhaled again, and I nodded, understanding. No more showing off. At least not right now.

The conversation stalled while we tidied everything away and cleaned up the small kitchen. For a moment, we had a normal life, and it felt as if we were an average family having a typical evening.

It ended when we sat down afterward. Ben pulled out a letter and passed it over to me. It was one I'd seen before.

"I still don't know what to do with this. We need to find a way to meet him, and I don't know if I can get us out of the city again, especially so soon. I've tried to answer him and see what he can do to come closer, but he's...elusive, and I haven't had another reply."

That wasn't the news I wanted to hear, but he was right. We had been walking a fine line. The elders were suspicious right now, and I couldn't blame them. Every time I left the city, I attracted trouble.

"What about Jace?" I asked a few minutes later when I handed the letter back.

"I'm not sure she likes us much. Well, she likes you, maybe. She thinks you're the heir, if nothing else."

"She brought us back to the car so we could come back here, and she seemed willing enough to help us." I shrugged, knowing she hadn't been my biggest fan and had appeared exasperated with me on more than one occasion.

Ben thought about it a little longer.

"There might be a way to make it work," he replied eventually. "She might not want to do it directly, but there were a fair few people in the cell she ran who clearly think you're the heir and need to be treated as such. They would probably do anything you asked as long as it wouldn't kill them."

"Possibly, but the only one we can reach without leaving the city is Jace by leaving something in the cave."

Again, Ben frowned, and the atmosphere between us grew more tense.

"What?" I asked. "I really think she'd be supportive. She helped us in the last fight. Stood beside us in a battle and helped us stay alive." Ben nodded as I spoke, and it helped calm me down again. He knew I was right.

"You're right that she helped us, and you could well be right that she's on our side and would do anything needed to aid you. But someone supporting you in a battle isn't the same as someone being beside you for a whole war. People are more nuanced than that. And she has her own agenda. Just as the leaders of her group do."

I sat back and thought about that for a minute, wondering how that might impact my thoughts on her. Did I trust her enough? And I realized I couldn't be sure. I *wanted* to trust people, but that wasn't the same as *actually* trusting them. I had always had trust issues, yet here I was, trying to trust anyone who helped me.

It wasn't like me to be so trusting, but it also wasn't like me to do a lot of the things I had been doing.

"I can't think of anyone else who can help us right now," I replied eventually. We both knew that it was partially a non-answer.

I couldn't be sure Jace was trustworthy, but neither could I be sure of anyone else. And I only had Anthony's word that I could trust Ben. So far, he'd not done anything to betray me, but by his own logic, that could change, and I could find myself betrayed.

"To be fair to your suggestion, she's still likely to be our best bet. But we'd need to contact her and get a message to her."

"I've got her phone number. She gave it to me the last time, and a burner to contact her on." I got up and rummaged through my bag for the phone inside.

It took a few minutes, but I eventually found it and pulled it out.

"Before I do this, are you as okay with it as you think you can be?" I asked, my fingers hovering over the keypad.

"We have no choice if we're going to make progress in our lifetimes. We need to find a way to get you safe. A way to get answers. In the last month or so, I've learned that the man I loved was keeping one of the biggest secrets he could from me, but that he didn't really want to. That he believed it was for my safety. That he was protecting what he thought was the only hope for our entire world to survive and that he knew you had no idea and would need me if he ever died or failed. And then, somehow, something went wrong."

"And now we're both muddling through and figuring this out the best we can." I tried to ignore the fear that made my heart pound at his words. It was all true, but it was scary. I didn't want to be anyone's hope. No part of me wanted to be anyone's savior. The responsibility was crushing.

I tried to compose myself and focus on what we needed to do. Jace was the only person who could help us with this next step without drawing too much attention to ourselves. The last thing I wanted right now was more attention. The few people who knew that I might be royalty were enough.

The events that had led to Anthony's death were also still a bit of a mystery, and I could only suspect that Fintar may have had something to do with it. After leading so many shadow catchers to attack me on our previous encounter, I was certain he had known all along that Anthony believed I was royalty and could unite the dragons to stop the gate from being broken.

Not sure what else to do, I asked Jace if she could meet our contact and get the information he had for us and them, and hoped it was the right call. Jace worked for what the elders would call a terrorist organization.

Everyone in the city believed that they were a terrorist cell. Anthony had worked with them despite this.

Our own discoveries had also led us to think that the group wasn't as bad as the city had made out. They'd helped us, saved our lives, and continued to share with me what they knew and why. For a group that operated in the shadows, they had been incredibly transparent to us on subjects that concerned me, especially since I'd earned their trust and fought shadow catchers beside them.

With the message sent to Jace, I sat back again and tried to calm down. It only took a minute or so before I had a response, and I tried to stay calm as I read it.

Will need more information. Meet after dark at the drop-off point.

I exhaled, remembering what had happened the last

time I was there. I'd hoped to avoid the beach and cave. But the truth was I wanted to avoid everything. I had been hiding in the city since I got back, going to lessons and spending time with my friends and hoping to never have to face any of it.

"Do you want me to come with you?" Ben asked when he noticed my reaction.

"It's possibly not wise. It puts you in danger too."

"But it gives you more power to draw on if the shadow catchers arrive again."

I frowned. It was a good point. The only problem with it was that to do anything but rebuff them, I needed multiple dragons of different colors. Somehow the combination of powers helped me to combat them. Alone, I could only stun them. I didn't think I could kill them without some very powerful dragons backing me up.

Of course, I didn't know exact numbers or how powerful, or what combinations were best. All I knew was that I was special and there was safety in numbers—to some degree.

Eventually, I nodded, and Ben grabbed a jacket.

"If anyone asks, I can say that I wanted to teach you something about the night sky, and we need to be a bit farther from the city." Ben grinned at me.

I got to my feet. "Let's hope there aren't any clouds."

There weren't, but I had only gone about fifteen yards from the front door of Ben's apartment and down a couple of floors when Flick flew down and landed beside me.

"Thought that was you. You two look as if you're on a mission. I'm bored, and so are most of the dragons who give you crap. I should probably come with you."

I opened my mouth to object, but I noticed the silhouette of another dragon before Neritas also transformed and landed on the bridge, although he wasn't quite as neat and wobbled it slightly.

"Evening," he added as he nodded at me and the others.

"Nothing I say will deter you two from coming with me wherever I'm going, will it?" I asked.

"Nope. Not even if you leave the city if it can be helped. You clearly need some extra protection, and we're probably the only other dragons here who think it's worth it, wherever this leads." Neritas smirked, and Flick looked as if this amused him too.

I had never been sure exactly what these two fellas' angle was, but I was always glad to have them at my side. It meant I was now leaving the city with three powerful dragons of different colors, and while I wasn't sure exactly what the combination of my red, Ben's blue, and their green and yellow would do, it gave me comfort.

Even Ben visibly relaxed when they fell in beside us. I didn't need to say anything to anyone as I led the way. This was one of those adventures where my companions knew I had the lead, and they were here for their own curiosity and feelings of duty and adventure.

Now I had to find out what Jace could do for me and if this benefactor knew who I was and why I was being paid so much money. But I didn't expect my journey to be so simple. So far, it had been anything but.

CHAPTER THREE

The wind blew across the shore, making me shudder as soon as I was out of the shadow of the furthest tower and nothing stood between me and the elements. My response was short-lived, however. Having learned how to fly at high altitudes, I had also learned how to let the dragon nature in me adjust my body temperature and keep me going.

Although being such a powerful dragon had some serious disadvantages—like being unwanted in the city—I could see the benefits and was grateful to have learned from my time here. I could tell I was a more powerful and more confident young woman than the day I had first arrived.

Some of that had come from having to survive some harrowing events, but the rest I had picked up from lessons and everything that the dragons in the city appeared to know instinctively. There was a lot to being a dragon, and I'd been on a steep learning curve so far.

I paused to make sure I was going in the right direction

while also taking the time to check my little posse was still with me and that no one else from the city was following. As far as I could tell, we were the only ones out there, and we were safe enough. No shadow catchers were in the area either.

Working out where we'd sat on the beach watching meteorites when I had gone to meet Jace in the cave, I retraced my steps.

"Ah, is this where you went that night?" Neritas asked when he noticed the path I was on.

"It is. I'm hoping to meet the same person I met then."

"A person?" Neritas was more surprised than I'd expected, and Flick raised his eyebrows and looked between me and Ben, the only one of the three of them who wasn't reacting.

"Well...a dragon. From somewhere else. She's been helping me find my family."

"Another dragon—who isn't from another city, or is?" Neritas stepped closer, his voice getting lower. For a fraction of a second, I felt afraid. Neritas was one of the dragons who was most intimidating to me, and I didn't want to make him angry in some way.

"They've stood beside me in battle, and they've been helping me. I don't know much more about them. I'm asking them for help again." It was all the explanation I could give him. I had to keep going and hope it was enough.

I tried to focus on my goal and turn my back on him for a moment, but it was easier said than done. I wasn't sure this was the right course of action, and as Ben had reminded me, I didn't know for sure that I could trust Jace. I didn't need anyone to tell me.

But I had no other option. I wanted answers. Trusting her was all I had to work with. I promised myself I'd be cautious, hence my current company. Even if I didn't trust Jace entirely, there was still merit to seeing what another person did with the information I couldn't act on.

I'd taken the same leap in telling Neritas and Flick about me and everything that had happened so far. They were now defending me more fiercely than ever, and I had to hope that it was enough to make sure we were okay and that I survived whatever was coming.

All these thoughts crowded my head as I traveled along the final section of the path toward the cave. I saw the silhouette of the opening on the edge of the cliff as we got closer and paused at the entrance.

"I need to go in there." I had met Jace inside last time. In the past, she'd come to drop off or pick up information, but I didn't have anything to give her that she didn't already have. This wasn't a swap. I needed her to go and do what I couldn't.

I took a deep breath and continued deeper in. Again my group came with me, my hand glowing faintly to light our way. Not wanting anyone to see it from the city, I kept it faint at first but let it shine a little brighter when I went around a natural bend in the cave structure.

A few minutes later, we were at the meeting point in the cave, and I looked over at the shelf where we normally left items for each other. It was empty, which was what I'd expected to see, but I wouldn't have been surprised either way. I didn't want to underestimate the organization that

Jace worked for. They might mean well, but it seemed as if they could do some pretty undesirable things.

Of course, I didn't know for sure. They could be amazing for all the truth I had on the matter. Ben hadn't told me more, and I kept forgetting to ask. It wasn't something I could look up alone. I'd tried that, looking at the history information in the public domain, but I couldn't look anywhere else without making it too obvious.

We stood around waiting as I tried to think where Jace might go. I'd had the foresight to bring with me the phone that would let me contact her, so I messaged her and let her know that we were at the rendezvous point. After several minutes, she still hadn't replied or turned up.

I tried not to panic, but the only other time she had been here, we had been attacked by shadow catchers, and I didn't want a repeat. I'd snuck out successfully and got the party to safety, but it had been tense. I didn't like to see shadow catchers so close to the city. Thankfully, the elders had never learned about that one.

And it was a good job that they hadn't. They were already growing suspicious about my actions and whereabouts whenever I left the city. I could only hide so much, and I felt compelled to do that because they'd had to help gloss over my first encounter with the monstrous creatures when I crash-landed in an LA park as a dragon—not an easy thing to cover up.

Feeling a sense of unease creep up the back of my neck, I closed my eyes to focus on the sensation and work out if I needed to get us out of the area. But I wasn't sure what it was I was feeling. It was strange compared to normal, but I tried not to let it get to me. I breathed deeply to keep calm.

I knew what the shadow catchers felt like, and it was clear that none were close by. This feeling was caused by something different. I was sure of it. I opted to head out of the caves when I still had no response from Jace over ten minutes later. If Jace was going to meet me, she'd be here already. The woman had never been this late.

We were still a little way from the exit of the cave when the funny feeling on the edge of my mind grew suddenly. Immediately, I stopped. Neritas and Flick crashed into the back of me, and the darkness and tensions made them both swear. Whatever this was, it wasn't helpful.

"Shadow catchers," I said to get their attention, hoping they noticed the same strange slithering sound that I did.

The creatures were in the cave with us and felt strange to my senses, cloaked somehow. I was almost certain that they hadn't been in here earlier. Or even close. Why were they so hard to track?

"We need to try and find another way out," I suggested as I walked deeper and in a direction I'd never explored. It wasn't a helpful statement. If there was another way out somewhere, I'd have found it. I didn't want to risk the lives of the folks with me if it could be helped.

On top of the danger, the two younger dragons who'd insisted on being by my side on this fool's errand might never have seen a shadow catcher up close. I was certain that they'd never fought one.

Ben was willing to rush down all the small nooks and any areas that looked like they might lead to another way out, and it didn't take long to confirm that there wasn't another way out. We could do nothing but face our foes.

"Stick close to me," I said. Neritas and Flick flanked me as closely as they dared.

It was an unnecessary statement. They were here to stay close and help keep me safe.

The only flaw with our plan was the lack of a shield or weapon. I had nothing to defend us with or to use against the shadow catchers.

Using my hand as a light, I looked around for any debris that might help. I couldn't find anything, but my companions all searched as well, joining me in trying to defend us.

In the end, Ben frowned and picked up what looked like a chunk of wooden debris. A strange branch that had washed up in here then dried out and collected dust ever since.

I took it from him, sure we wouldn't find anything better. It was only a few seconds before the shadow catchers closed the gap between us and them. I'd been able to feel them following our scent and path. They sniffed as they went, with the bodies of slithering snakes, heads of lions, and bird beaks.

And they were slightly translucent, which was probably the scariest element. Their appearance alone was a sight that was terrifying in and of itself. It worried me that Neritas and Flick had never seen one of these creatures before. How would they react?

I'd heard that some dragons froze in fear, and most had no defense against them. And I'd also met someone who could control these creatures before, someone who had proclaimed himself a friend but turned out to be the opposite. Fintar had tricked all of us.

While dragons healed faster than most humans, and the wounds I'd received on my hands from grabbing the handler of the last shadow catchers I'd encountered had healed well, my hands had been partially protected. Something about my powers seemed to counteract Fintar's.

I put my finger to my lips and dimmed the light I was providing more as Ben encouraged Neritas and Flick to stand behind me. They didn't seem to want to, resisting the notion of leaving me in front, but I turned from them and shuffled forward anyway, clutching a wide piece of driftwood I'd found as a makeshift shield and Ben's stick as a sword.

As the first shadow catcher came around the corner, I heard Flick gasp. Neritas moved to get between me and it, but Ben stopped him, and I moved back over in front. A moment later, Ben put his hand on my shoulder, and Neritas and Flick did the same.

Without any of us saying anything, I hoped that Ben was encouraging them to initiate contact with me. Hopefully, they would keep touching and following me, even when I drew on their power. It scared me to be facing such danger alongside dragons who had never been taught about it, and I regretted not educating them sooner, but hindsight is a wonderful thing. Regardless, I had to try to save us all.

We had no way past the shadow catcher in front of me, and it would detect us soon anyway. I took a slow step forward. At first, the people with me didn't follow, and I lost contact with them, but their hands returned to my shoulders soon, and I pulled on all of our powers.

With just the single enemy in the cave with us and the

sense that there weren't many nearby, I didn't feel the need to use their power to bolster myself, so I was gentle and only charged the wood I held in each hand.

As the monster caught our scent finally and let out its usual screech of finding its prey, I lashed out. Before it could adjust to what was in front of it, I stuffed the stick deep in its flesh.

I didn't know if it was enough to kill it, but the creature reeled back, and I kept the power flowing through the stick, trying to hold the charge in it constant rather than let it dissipate. I drew more power from my companions, but they kept contact and moved with me this time.

I lunged again, trying to get the creature to fall back deeper into the cave and leave our exit free. It let out another pained cry as the stick drove deep, but I pulled it out fast and smacked it with the wider panel. It slid backward and seemed to pant and swish its head back and forth as if it couldn't continue.

"Time to run." I backed up and drew on their power one last time to charge the weaponry and shield again. They were makeshift but serving well enough now that I was getting an idea of how to protect and stop them from decaying.

As my friends turned to run, I backed up with them, keeping an eye on the shadow catcher to make sure it didn't follow too easily. Water flowed across the cave floor toward it—the monster was trying to heal itself and regain its energy.

Comforted by its behavior, I spun and ran after my friends, lighting us up more to get us out without falling. It didn't take long before we were out on the beach again.

Ben led us back down the path and away from the city, a strategy we had used in the past, but he stopped when he came close to another demon that had been lying in wait. Although I could feel them, I had been so focused on the charge in my weapons and how my friends were reacting that I hadn't been keeping track of them.

I hurried past Flick, almost tripping over him, but he and Ben helped catch me. The shadow catcher lunged, but I managed to block the attack with the driftwood. The charge quickly drained, and the wood started to rot as I stabbed at the shadow catcher.

The monster yelped in pain, but unlike those before it, it did not reel back. Fear made my heart race, but I drew again on the power in myself and my friends, stepping back and into them. It gave me some space to recover, but the shield was almost entirely decimated this time. I stabbed again and again as swiftly as I could.

Hitting it once more seemed to finally deter the creature, and it backed up a little. It still didn't run, and despite my efforts, the stick I was using as a sword was also starting to decay from the shadow catchers' natural ability to fill everything they touched with rot and fungus. It could make for some disgusting sights.

Ben leaned in to whisper. "You've got this."

Not able to spare the thought to respond verbally, I sucked a little more power from all of them and dodged the monster's beak before I stabbed into the side of it again.

My weapon hit right in its side, getting in deep, as my companions also moved to get behind me again and out of harm's way. I felt lightning crackle at the same time, and the air warmed around me. We were all using our abilities. It was only the combination of our powers that would help, though.

A new attack from me only scraped the beast's shoulder region, but it elicited another cry, and the creature flinched to one side again. Now it felt like I was hurting the monster. I wasn't completely drained, so I was able to charge the stick again quickly and jab it back into the creature. Its beak missed me by millimeters when I struck again.

Finally, it appeared to falter, wounded and sliding to one side. I considered encouraging everyone to run, but they were still all close, and a glance showed set jaws and determined expressions. Instead of fleeing, I charged the weapon and what was left of the shield once more and hit the creature with both.

The loudest squeal of all sounded through the night, and the creature listed farther to one side. I charged and struck for the final time, and the shadow catcher seemed to pop and disappear.

I exhaled, knowing the danger wasn't over, but hearing the gasps of surprise from my younger companions.

"Is that dead?" Flick asked.

"We think so, but we need to keep moving. The one in the cave will follow shortly." Ben encouraged us all back down the path, and I had no objection.

I dropped the shield I carried as we hurried away into the ocean, letting the waves cover our sounds for now.

"That was crazy." Neritas ran his hand through his hair while we all relaxed for a moment. "And it wasn't the first time you've killed one of those things, was it?"

I shook my head and felt outward with my mind for the first monster we'd fought. It had come out of the cave, but instead of coming after us, it had moved north and away from the city. We were safe, and so was everyone in the city.

CHAPTER FOUR

No one said anything after getting out of the ocean and back into the city proper, not until we were all sitting around the table in Ben's apartment.

Ben gave everyone a hot drink and joined us. "We can't keep doing this." All of us had towels, and he'd heated the air a little, too.

I shook. I was drained and tired, and he didn't need to tell me that it was all too much.

"How many times have you killed shadow catchers?" Flick asked.

I decided to be honest. "Only on two separate occasions. But I've fought them many times. I think I need to draw on the power of more dragons to kill them."

I tried to read their expressions. I was worried about their reactions to having me pull on their power, but it seemed neither of them would speak of it without some nudging.

Ben spoke up. "I know it's weird having Scarlet draw on

your magic, but it's a trait of red dragons, as far as we can tell."

"Or a trait of royal dragons," Neritas added, looking at Ben before looking back at me.

"Possibly. Possibly not." I met his gaze, not sure what the expression on his face meant and feeling a little afraid under its scrutiny. This evening had not gone according to plan, and I didn't know how to explain it to my friends or be sure of their reaction.

"How do you do this?" Flick leaned forward. "How do you survive all these encounters and then just come back to the city and go to lessons and try to fit in? This is insane. You must struggle so much not to claim the throne and order all these bullies to be punished."

Ben let out a chuckle before I could respond. "She doesn't want a throne, and there's still a lot more unknowns."

"I have no proof that would convince anyone. And I'm not sure I even want to. Until a month or so ago, I was just living my life and being normal. I want to get back to that."

"You're never going to be able to. Red dragons don't get peace." Neritas lifted his chin, still studying me.

"I'd complain about how unfair that is, but there doesn't seem to be much point. It's not going to change the color of my scales."

It was silent after I spoke, and my mind turned from what they thought of what had happened to what on earth I was going to do. If they weren't coping well with such encounters, I'd see it in them when the adrenaline wore off. It was urgent to figure out my next action.

"Why are the shadow catchers lurking everywhere you

go?" Flick asked a few minutes later.

I took the final gulp of my tea and frowned.

"No idea. Not for sure. A handler we ran into was sending them after me, we learned, but they appeared to act differently when he was nearby. I just seem to attract them."

"They're probably all around the city. They know there aren't many routes out. You'll be hounded any time you're outside the city limits for long. You need to learn to fight. You need weapons." Neritas crossed his arms over his chest.

"And where am I going to get those? I'd have to join the guard to get a shield, and almost none of them have any weapons. This isn't a city with an army of any kind. Most dragons think there's no way to hurt, let alone kill, a demon."

Flick suddenly moved and opened his mouth as if to speak, then closed it, tipped his head to the side for a second, and also crossed his arms.

"What happened to the information we're being taught? If this is possible, how do we not know?" Flick asked, speaking the words slowly as if he was still considering them while he spoke. "Surely red dragons have been doing this for years. There's so many parts of our history and lessons in various different classes that would have to be rewritten for this to be covered up."

"Yes, which means someone in this city doesn't want anyone to know what red dragons are capable of or that dragons uniting with red leaders can achieve much more powerful things," Ben explained again.

"And we don't know everything I might be capable of.

Or all of you. We're having to rediscover history and information and skills…"

"Which is what you've been doing when you leave the city and what your contact who was meant to show today is helping with?" Neritas didn't look away from me.

I felt a flush of heat in my cheeks under all his scrutiny. I had no idea what it meant, but I nodded in response to his question. It reminded me that Jace hadn't shown up, but if the shadow catchers had got there before her, she might not have had any choice. Although I didn't want Neritas and Flick to know too much, I got the phone and sent Jace another message asking her if she was okay.

After tucking it into my pocket, I got up and moved to the kitchen counter to get some snacks. I had a feeling we were all going to be here a while longer. No one wanted to leave, and I wasn't going to kick my friends out. I could only hope Ben understood.

"What if I could get you an actual weapon and a shield?" Neritas offered once I sat back down with chips and dip.

"Then we could help you train and practice. I don't know about Neritas, but it felt pretty weird having you pull magical energy from us, but also cool to see what we were capable of being used for more than the party tricks we were doing in lessons the other day."

"Lessons Scarlet has graduated from," Ben added.

"You mean kicked out for showing off and intimidating all my classmates," I replied.

"You said it, not me."

I chuckled, unable to help it and grateful that Ben wasn't cross with me for that. We both knew that I wasn't perfect, and I was a hotheaded red dragon sometimes too.

Although I tried not to live up to the stereotype of the red dragons before me, I knew I had their temperament to some degree.

"That presents one small problem. We can't protect you when we're in different classes." Neritas crunched a chip when he finished speaking.

"I've already insisted that I take over teaching Scarlet during that session," Ben reassured Neritas. "I'm going to make sure she's got me or you around for now. At least until we can figure out what the hell is going on."

"Did Anthony know?" Flick asked.

"Maybe. He knew some things—we've learned from his diary—but we're still following leads he was following and trying to find out everything he'd uncovered."

Everyone nodded, and silence fell again. I missed him so much still. I could never hear his name without the seriousness of losing him and what happened in his last days hitting me to my core.

Neritas got up and encouraged Flick to do the same. He came over to me and hugged me. It took me by surprise, but I ended up hugging them both, and even Ben joined in.

Neritas gave my arm a squeeze.

"We'll figure out a way through all this together. You're not alone, and people care about you, Scarlet. Whoever you're related to and whatever is happening. You didn't ask for any of this, and you're handling it a lot better than I think Flick or I would." Neritas gave my arm a squeeze.

"Tomorrow, we start training. No arguments. Let's figure out what you're capable of and work out how to defend this city if needed." Flick looked serious and determined, his jaw set.

Their attitude gave me some hope. It wasn't much of a plan, and I still had no idea what I was going to truly do long term, but it was enough for now.

"You'll need to be careful if you train," Ben said when the door was shut again. "I won't be able to join you, and if you get caught..."

"I know. It could blow everything wide open, but I get the feeling that I need to learn as much as I can as fast as I can. Because these things aren't leaving me alone, and Neritas is right. It's as if they're lurking around the city and just waiting for me to show up."

My phone vibrating disturbed me from the conversation. It was a message from Jace, and I swiftly read it, grateful to note that she was still alive.

> **Couldn't make it. Sorry. I got caught up. Roads not clear and I think that Fintar is nearby. Be careful. Keep yourself alive and don't take risks that you don't need to.**

I paused, not sure how to respond. The concern for me felt strange when her lack of communication prior to me getting to the cave had put me in danger, but I also knew that if Jace had run into shadow catchers, she would have been in far more trouble than I would have. I could defend myself against them—even against the handler—but she couldn't.

"I think it's time to work out how to do this ourselves," I told Ben. "Go meet our contact and not put anyone else in danger."

"You want me to figure out how to get us out of the city

again?" Ben asked, exhaling and sinking into an armchair.

"Do we have any choice? Jace can't get to us to get the information she needs, and I don't like asking her to walk into danger when she can't defend herself." I sat opposite him, still not tired but knowing that I needed some rest. I was drained from the fight and working out how to get past the shadow catchers.

When I had a dragon of every color with me and spares, it had been easier to hurt the shadow catchers, and killing them had been a pleasant surprise, but it had been different when having to make sure the three dragons I cared about didn't get hurt. It also hadn't helped to have no weapon.

Neritas seemed to be willing to help on that score in the future, however. A part of me wanted to know how on earth he felt he could do that for me, but I also knew he was a bit of a bad boy and might have a past he didn't want to talk about. His reaction and support had been the opposite of what Ben had expected of him originally.

"I don't like any of this." Ben shook his head.

"I don't think either of us have since the beginning. But we need our answers and proof. Will you write to our contact again?"

He met my gaze finally before nodding. It was settled. We would think of a way to get me out of the city. In the meantime, I would train and keep learning. I had a flight lesson the following day to look forward to, and I would need to be at my best.

Not sure what else to do and aware that Ben was probably hurting and missing Anthony as well, I decided to head to bed and let him get some rest. Somehow, we'd make Anthony's death mean something. I had to.

CHAPTER FIVE

The wind whistled past my scales as I flew through the air. I was flanked by the usual dragons—my teacher, the two black guards, and Neritas and Flick keeping formation ahead and around me. It was a flight pattern I was used to. Flying also gave me the chance to practice talking in the heads of the others and blocking out voices I didn't want to hear.

Sometimes the dragons who didn't like me tried to get into my head. And I had to fly while holding them out. It was good for me.

Despite all the challenges, flying was my favorite thing to do. My favorite lessons, my favorite teacher, and all the best moments in the city. I was being pushed hard, and sometimes even Neritas and the guards struggled to keep up, but Flick was always with me, and the teacher never appeared to struggle to fly, no matter what he asked me to do.

Today we were trying more difficult flying techniques. Quick changes in directions and changes to speeds and styles of flying. In a lot of ways, it was fun, but it was challenging.

I banked hard near a tower and clipped the stonework with the tip of my wing. It stung, but it was a reminder to focus again. The next few orders I was given, I executed perfectly, with my teacher out in front enough that I could also read his flight pattern and shift in body and wings to get an idea of what I was expected to do next.

All right, I think we're done for today, my teacher said into our heads before he gently pulled up and guided us among the towers of the city and back toward the platform we had launched from. I followed, feeling both sadness to know the lesson was at its end and a thrill of excitement at what I knew was going to follow soon.

It wasn't long before sunset, and my companions and I had already agreed that we were going to get some dinner and then go somewhere quiet outside the city when it was dark. There we would begin our first training session.

Although Neritas had said no more about it, I was also expecting that he would show me what weapons and shields he had acquired. Either way, I was looking forward to it.

I landed on the platform and almost immediately transformed into a human. Both of my friends could do both at the same time, but I still preferred to do one and then the other.

Once we were all back in human form, I smiled at Jared.

"Again, you continue to learn fast and outshine many others, Scarlet. There isn't much more that I can teach you, but I'd be honored if you'd continue to come to my lessons as often as you have and let me hone your skills a little more here and there."

"If you feel you can teach me anything, no matter how small, then I will continue to be here when you require."

"Fantastic." He broke into a broad grin and let me head back down the stairs.

Without a word between us, Neritas, Flick, and I went toward our favorite place to eat dinner and found a table out of the way. It wasn't busy yet, since our flying lesson had finished a little early and the tower was near enough to the restaurant that we didn't have far to go.

I could barely sit still, but I tried to look normal as more and more dragons appeared and Flick went to order for us. I stayed with Neritas and tried to think of anything to say to take my mind off later.

Neritas leaned in closer and lowered his voice. "You're really a royal, aren't you?"

"I don't know," I replied. "It's possible."

"I know you don't want to be. And I can't say I blame you. But you need to own who you are. I don't normally give a crap about anyone, and I don't care about the elders and the way they run this city. You have given me faith again. You've made it clear that there's more to this life than living in this city for centuries while the world evolves around us."

"You want to do things differently?" I asked, deflecting it back at him.

He shifted his lower jaw to one side and thought about my question.

"Yes, but with no agenda. I don't like the current one, but I don't know what would be better. We don't have enough information. We don't know what's actually needed yet. But I do know you. You're a red dragon with a passion for protecting people. Your anger and passion will make you formidable. It already is making you formidable."

"But it doesn't give me the right."

"No one ever has the right, but someone has to step up to the job. I mean it. I've never been willing to follow anyone's lead, but you know what you're doing, and you care enough. Anthony believed in you. Ben believes in you, and you've been protected for your entire life in the hope that you can save us all. I'm no fool. I want you on a throne, and I'll do what I can to make it happen."

"What if it's not what I want?"

"The fact that you don't want it makes you perfect."

"Everyone always says that." I frowned and shook my head. "I don't want anyone to get hurt. I don't want to get hurt. But it looks as if I'm not going to get much choice. As far as we know, I am the only red dragon left, and a red dragon is needed to reinforce the gate. If nothing else, I need to help save the entire world."

"Then I'll help you get on the throne. And I'll fight at your side however I can."

"Thank you," I replied, not sure what else to say. The seriousness of the whole conversation was too much for me, and I wanted to only think about the next step, not about some end goal. I wanted to train to keep myself and those I cared about safe, and I wanted to find out what I could about my parents.

Everything else could wait for another day.

Thankfully Flick came back with our food, and this stopped the conversation. I knew it wasn't quite done, but

Neritas didn't seem to want to talk about it when we weren't alone, and I wasn't going to bring it up again. No part of me wanted the pressure to take a throne and change a city or culture that had been in place for centuries.

I ate slowly, despite my eagerness to train. Now that it was coming to it, I was nervous and not sure I wanted to do it. We would be attacked again, not to mention the risks we would take in sneaking out of the city once again. I was already in trouble with the elders, and many of the city dragons looked down on me. Having them think even less of me or think me even more of a rebel and troublemaker wouldn't help change their perception of me.

It wasn't the first time my two companions had offered to help me learn to use my abilities, but it was the first time they had seen how badly I needed it. Given they had been in danger as well, I couldn't blame them for being eager.

By the time I had finished eating, it was finally dark, and my companions were shuffling with impatience. It only then occurred to me that they might both be nervous too. The prior evening was possibly the first time either of them had ever been in any danger, and they had volunteered to come out with me again regularly to train and face that danger every time.

I hadn't been sensitive enough to what it meant for them, and I could have kicked myself for not picking up on it.

"Let's go." I smiled at both of them and hoped to reassure them with my confidence.

Either they hid their nerves better once we were moving, or my own demeanor had helped them, because they settled down with me and we made our way all the way to the bottom level of the city and where it connected to the beach. In order to protect its inhabitants from shadow catchers, the city had been built out over the water, but a few narrow bridges and a small road connected it to the mainland. All of it was hidden from humans, but we could all see it as we headed out.

I went first, not wanting the others to walk into danger. Both of them came in close behind me, and I instantly felt grateful. I wasn't sure that the two of them combined with my own power would be enough for us to kill any shadow catchers if they showed up, but they would be enough to help me repel them and get us safely back to the city or into the ocean.

As we walked, we looked out for other dragons, hoping not to be seen. To give us a better chance at stealth, we took a smaller route that curled around a small civilian tower.

I felt for demons nearby, wanting to make sure it was going to at least be safe for the beginning of my lesson, and then I stepped down onto the sand. We were close to the shoreline, and the tide was high and noisy enough to cover our footsteps. Neritas ducked down and reached under the edge of the bridge.

Pulling out something wrapped in cloth, he flicked me a wink.

"Got you a little present."

Neritas opened up the cloth to reveal a large shield, identical to the ones the guards in the city used, and a sword. I'd never seen a weapon quite like it and gravitated toward it. As I took hold of the hilt, it was as if something in it activated. A line inlaid into the handle lit up, and the trail spread all the way down to the tip of the sword.

Neritas' eyes widened. "It didn't do that before."

I lifted it up, feeling the weight of it as it drew slightly on my power. It felt natural to hold and magically connect to. The lines continued to light up until a pattern shone all the way from the handle to the tip of the blade. It was faint but bright enough that my hand and the air around it glowed slightly.

"Where did you get this?" Flick asked, speaking the question forming in my mind.

"Let's just say that in my wilder days as a young dragon, I found a lot of things I shouldn't have and picked a few locks to get to them. Given what we know of Scarlet, this seemed...fitting."

"You stole this from some royal stash?" I asked.

Neritas didn't reply, but I saw the corner of his mouth twitch up.

He changed the subject. "Can you make it brighter or darken it?"

The thought hadn't occurred to me, but I concentrated, and it shone a little brighter, lighting up the three of us. I didn't keep it that way but made it darker again until the lines were so faint that they made the sword look decorated without casting any light anywhere else.

"Perfect." Neritas smiled again, clearly pleased with what he'd provided.

"It's easier than the pattern I made on the shield the other day." I slowly moved it around and got a feel for holding it. I wasn't sure if I was wielding it right, but it didn't feel particularly heavy or difficult to thrust with.

The metal seemed to gleam, and it looked sharper than any sword I'd ever seen. As I swished it around, the others backed up a little and gave me some space. I reached for the shield and slipped that onto my arm so I could try wielding both together. It felt good to have something so well-made in my hands.

I stepped a little farther away to figure out how we could train and learn to defend ourselves together, determined to work with the others to see if they could help themselves as well.

Since the previous conversation about the lessons not teaching us everything we needed to know regarding the predicament of the entire dragon race, I had wondered if Flick and Neritas might be able to do more than they realized too. It was worth trying to find out.

We were still walking away, the sand crunching beneath our feet, when a sound from behind made us all turn around fast. I lifted the sword and instinctively made it shine brighter.

It lit up the human form of a familiar dragon. Capricia, the head guard of the city. I had fought shadow catchers alongside her in the past. This wasn't good. Although the dragons could come out onto this beach, she would know we were up to something illegal, or at the very least objectionable, and we'd barely been out here for five minutes.

Without saying a word, she looked around to check that the coast was clear. Her own shield rested on one arm in front of her. When she was satisfied it was safe, she came closer and I dimmed the light again to keep us illuminated but not draw any more attention to us.

"This is a little...unconventional, isn't it?" Her voice was quieter than I expected.

"It is." I met her gaze, not intending to explain unless I had to. My heart raced, but Neritas and Flick had fallen in behind me, and Capricia looked between them and me for a moment.

"Is this some kind of training exercise?" she asked.

"Something like that."

"If it was anyone else out here, I'd feel as if I needed to tell your legal guardians and make sure that they were informed of your behavior. But I'm pretty sure one of them knows, one of you doesn't have any, and the other has one who doesn't care unless it impacts her social life. Nothing will happen if I do, will it?"

"No," Flick and Neritas replied as I shook my head.

I felt a chill run through me at the information in this statement. Although I had spent a lot of time with my two companions, we had almost exclusively talked about me or current affairs and lessons. Neither of them had volunteered much information about themselves. Had I missed the fact that both of them had far less-than-ideal home lives?

"Okay. I know what Scarlet here is up against and the dangers she has faced in the past, so I'm going to allow this on one condition, is that clear?"

"What's the condition?" I shot back, knowing I sounded more antagonistic than I needed to.

"I will keep an eye on you three and help keep you safe."

I exhaled, not entirely sure I liked the condition but feeling the genuine gesture in her words.

"Accepted," Neritas said before Flick or I could respond.

Glancing at him, I wondered what he was thinking. I knew it was unlikely that we could argue with her condition, but I hadn't been ready to agree to it right away.

"And I would offer my services in teaching you how to use that thing," she added, bringing my attention back to her.

"All right," I replied. This wasn't what I'd expected, but if I could get more help and it might save a life, I was willing to take the risk. After all, Capricia had kept a secret of mine in the past, something to give me some faith in her.

CHAPTER SIX

After our interruption, it took me a moment to focus again. Capricia had gone back toward the city after correcting my grip on the sword and giving Neritas her shield so I could attack without hurting him.

It allowed the three of us to settle back into our usual companionship, although we were all now aware of being watched. Most of the pressure was on me, and not them, to perform and use my magic. Magic that almost no one in the city thought was possible.

I took a few deep breaths and squared up to Neritas. None of us knew where to begin, but any practice would help. I tried to work out how to attack Neritas with the sword. He laughed when I lunged slowly, and he easily dodged.

"We should watch some internet videos or something," Flick pointed out.

I chuckled, and Neritas grinned. "It might help."

"Okay, let's come back to that part then and focus on the magic side of things instead," I suggested.

Neritas nodded, and both he and Flick came in closer so I could draw on their power. In the past, I'd drawn on the powers of dragons without direct contact, although they'd needed to be nearby, so I tried that now before they put hands on my shoulders.

At first, it didn't seem to work, but soon I felt the familiar feeling of being able to draw on their power, like pulling on toffee and stretching it out. I was gentle, aware it might not be a good feeling for them.

I had felt as if I had run out on a previous occasion, and I knew we had used our powers here and there throughout the day. Draining them completely wouldn't be kind, especially while we were somewhere dangerous and the shadow catchers could reach us. My powers could only do so much for us, and my conscience wouldn't let me put them in too much danger, even if they understood it and were willing.

Pulling in more power, I charged the sword and shield. I couldn't make it harder in the same way that I could when I pulled on the abilities of a black dragon, but electricity crackled across its surface, and I felt the weapon filling with magic in a way that nothing else ever had. It was almost as if it had a magic storage battery in it.

I stopped, not sure what to do. If this could store energy, it made sense to fill it a little, but not if it was hard to use again or if I was fueling something I didn't understand.

Frowning, I lowered it and tried to figure out what it was doing, pointing it out to my companions. They looked at each other, and Neritas reached out to touch it.

Nothing happened, but he raised his eyebrows.

"Do you think it could enhance your abilities?"

"Maybe, but if it can, how was it made? There's nothing in any of the lessons I've had about magical artifacts of any kind. I know that magic can be used to make objects the human world can't, but not that they have any magical properties of their own. How does this shield store any magic?"

Neritas shrugged.

"Try and use it. Let's see what happens when you try and stab something."

Flick hung back a little now that everything was charged and I didn't need to draw from him. I focused on Neritas. I hesitated before I lashed out at his shield, making sure my magic was connected to the sword and it remained charged.

Although I did it slowly again, it was almost as if something slowed Neritas as well, and he only just blocked it in time. The real surprise was when the sword hit the metal. It sliced through it as if it were butter, cutting it in half and leaving Neritas holding two sections of it.

I gasped and pulled back.

"It shouldn't have done that. It didn't the last time."

"No. Before you charged it, it didn't do that at all."

"So, magic makes it better?" Flick asked.

"Sort of." I frowned as I looked at the shield and the sword again. I had a feeling that Capricia wasn't going to be happy about it. We'd inexplicably cut her shield in half, and I had no idea if it could be put back together or not.

Also, if this sword could cut through anything and nothing could keep any sparring partner safe, it would make training with it difficult. I was at a loss.

"Can you charge the shield?" Flick asked.

"Not the way I charged the sword." It was a good thought, but not something I could do without knowing how the sword worked.

"There was a shield and other stuff in the same place as the sword." Neritas took off the remnants of Capricia's shield and dropped them onto the sand.

"We might need you to go back and see what else you can take." Flick looked around and then sat.

"I don't know how I feel about you stealing for me." I picked up the pieces of the shield and tried to power down the sword and make the lights go out. It felt as if the lesson was done for the day. I wasn't sure I wanted to test anything more without knowing what was happening.

Encouraging the others to go back to the city with me, I started walking in that direction. As I did, I noticed the familiar feeling of unease off to one side on the land and away from the city. It wasn't strong, but it made me aware that shadow catchers were nearby.

"It's not safe out here anymore," I said, so my companions would understand that we needed to hurry.

As we reached Capricia, I encouraged her to head back into the city and raise the bridge after us to make sure the shadow catchers couldn't follow us. Capricia didn't appear happy about it.

"I want to know how you can see these things before the rest of us. Do you have super sight or something?" she asked.

"No. I can sense them. There's two coming this way, and they'll follow my scent if you don't pull up the bridge." I stared her in the face, hoping she'd not make me argue or prove it, but she only nodded and backed up, letting the three of us help her pull up the bridge and take away the path the shadow catchers could use.

I backed up and made the area around us darker almost instinctively. It didn't take too long for the shadow catchers to appear. They went straight to the patch of sand we had been standing on and training. None of us dared to move or speak as they sniffed around and came toward the city.

It took several more minutes for them to get to the end of the trail and find that it cut off abruptly. They sniffed at the air, but we were far enough away, and the city had so many smells and scents that ours didn't stand out.

They tried to find us for several minutes, circling and moving out a little from the spot where our trail ended, but nothing brought them directly to us, and the city was quiet enough behind us that they didn't pick up on it. We all slowly relaxed, our shoulders lowering and our breathing growing calmer until the shadow catchers were beyond sight again.

"Let's get back into the city proper. I'll lower this bridge again in an hour or so on my next walk around the city." Capricia turned to walk away as I lifted the darkness from around us.

Finally noticing the pieces of shield, she stopped again and stared.

"Sorry," I said as I handed it back.

"What the hell did you do to it?" She slowly took the two halves back and looked at them with her mouth slightly open and a disgusted look on her face. She inspected the cut.

"Let's just say that magic and a funky sword had an interesting result, and we probably shouldn't borrow your shield again. Can you fix it?" I asked.

She looked between me and it a couple of times.

"I'll say you shouldn't borrow it again. Are you trying to get me in trouble?"

I shook my head, not sure what else to say. I didn't want to say anything that could make it worse. I needed her to accept me and be okay with us sneaking out of the city to train more. Breaking her shield wasn't going to help my case.

"Okay, I think all three of you should go somewhere safe and study or something and keep yourselves out of any more trouble or mischief for the rest of the night. Do you hear me?"

"Of course, ma'am," Neritas replied and gently ushered me away.

We wrapped up the sword as Neritas offered the shield he'd taken to Capricia instead. She shook her head in disbelief as if she was still appalled at her own behavior, but the gesture seemed to soften her, and she took the shield and put it on her arm where her previous one had been.

Not sure what else to do, I tried to carry the sword back to Ben's without making it obvious what I was carrying. Thankfully, it was late enough that most of the city was quiet and the vast majority of the dragons still flying around weren't paying much attention to us.

To be extra careful, I added some subtle darkness around me and the item to make it harder to identify it. There was something about it that I felt as if I needed to hide. But I was also eager and excited to show Ben. I knew that he'd be fascinated by the sword. That it even existed was huge.

Thankfully, we weren't too far from Ben's apartment, and Neritas and Flick didn't stick around once they'd escorted me there.

"I know Capricia said to stay out of trouble, but I'm going to go see if I can find something like a shield that goes with that sword. If I find something, I'll bring it straight here."

"Thank you," I whispered back, considering hugging him.

Although I decided not to and took a step back and moved deeper into the room, Neritas wouldn't have given me the chance anyway. He turned and slipped away with Flick. The latter dragon took his larger form and flew up to his own tower, leaving my thief to wander into the night.

"How did it go?" Ben asked from his seat by the desk. He had his journals open and was clearly back at the task of trying to translate Anthony's coded messages some more.

I didn't respond to his questioning but moved over to him as I let go of the darkness I'd shrouded the weapon in and put the wrapped item on his desk. Still not speaking, I unwrapped it before his eyes.

He gaped at it as I touched the hilt and made the lines brighten.

"Where did you get this?"

"I'd get Neritas in trouble if I told you exactly, so let's just say that it was in the city and may technically already belong to me. It definitely responded to me trying to charge it, and it stores my power somehow. It also cut clean through one of the shields the city guards use once it was charged."

I spent the next few minutes explaining everything that had happened that evening to Ben and trying to get him to weigh in with an explanation. As I'd expected, he was fascinated.

More than once, I wielded it for him. A wooden plate he hadn't liked much and a few other items of little value but varying materials lay in pieces by the time he was satisfied with what he saw. It barely drained the sword. The blade felt as if it not only held the power inside it but ensured it was using the magic efficiently.

If this was something that my ancestors had used, I was starting to understand how they might have faced a horde of demons in battle and fought back the devil himself. It wasn't so hard with the right tools.

"I'm guessing this wasn't the only item there that you could possibly use?" Ben asked, and I shook my head and explained that Neritas was hoping to find something like a shield to go with it.

Although I considered that it might have been better if I went with the rogue to pilfer from the stash he'd found, there was an extra chance we'd get caught. I wanted to help identify what was most useful, but my presence alone and the interest the other dragons were taking in me increased the risk too much.

Exhausted, I sank into one of the chairs.

"For everything that you've achieved the last few days,

you seem pretty flat," Ben said as he sat, moving past the sword point I was being slightly careless with.

"I didn't achieve what I wanted. We still haven't met this guy and found out what he knows. I haven't really trained. I'm being kicked out of lessons and told I'm learning as much as there is, as if there's nothing left to know when there's clearly masses. And I have no easy way forward."

Ben shifted his jaw and then looked me in the face.

"It doesn't always look as if what is happening is progress, but several of the things you've mentioned are progress of a sort. We know that Jace can't help us. That between your two friends and me, there is enough power to kill a shadow catcher. That there's a sword designed for your powers. And you've gained time from classes you've finished."

When Ben put it like that, it didn't seem so bad, but I still didn't feel like things were working. It was time to take matters into our own hands.

Before I could say this, there was a gentle tap on the door. Back on his feet faster than me, Ben went to open it and revealed Neritas.

Without waiting for an invite, he strode inside and pulled back his coat. He carried a large shield made of a similar material to those of the guards of the city, but which also carried the same lines the sword did, was bigger, and somehow drew the eyes toward it.

"I believe this also belongs to you. Or close enough." A grin spread across his face and lit up his eyes.

As soon as I took it off him, I felt the connection in much the same way as the sword. It was also lighter than the shield I'd used earlier and sat more naturally on my arm.

"Thank you," I said. My words almost caught in my throat as I held both. I felt different with these. It helped, and I needed the help right now.

Neritas didn't stick around, disappearing back into the night again and leaving me with Ben once more.

"Get some sleep. I'll contact this guy again and see if I can set up a meeting." Ben gave my shoulder a squeeze, and I headed through to the bedroom with the sword and shield.

I'd try them out another day when I wasn't already tired and drained. I didn't think it would be a good idea to test something new right now. I'd broken enough today.

CHAPTER SEVEN

Capricia didn't look pleased to see me two evenings later when we dared to sneak out of the city again. She had been waiting for us by the same exit, but in the dark, where she wouldn't be noticed.

Although I appreciated that she was keeping our secret and she was helping to keep us safe, I wasn't sure how I felt about having her watch everything. For now, I couldn't think of a better alternative, however, and I hoped the little trust she was already earning wasn't misplaced.

Neritas winked at her as we went past, and Flick grinned. I focused on keeping my sword and shield hidden so that no one in the city saw it, but I flashed the shield at Capricia from under the sweatshirt I was carrying over it.

Her eyes went wide, but I noticed she clutched her own shield a little tighter.

"I shouldn't need to borrow yours this time," I said, grinning.

"Try not to break that one," she replied and returned the gesture.

It helped break some of the tension. I was pretty sure that the shield and sword were made for each other and that one wouldn't break the other, but I planned to be careful and test this theory first. There was no way I was risking such an amazing shield.

Once we were out on the sand in the dark and I had checked that we were as safe as we could be, I made the sky between us and the city a little darker to conceal us, and we got into position.

I slowly focused on the shield like I had with the sword and charged it up. It was just as easy, and the lines on it were soon glowing. Although they looked amazing, I made sure that they were dull and didn't make us easy to see before I handed the shield to Neritas.

Flick almost immediately backed up, a smirk flashing across his face.

"I'm not taking any chances with that sword," Flick explained. He continued to back up.

"Think yourself grateful that you weren't the one holding the shield last time," Neritas replied. He sounded grumpy about it, but his eyes shone as if he was amused.

Either way, I was going to make sure that he wasn't in any danger this time. I concentrated on connecting to the sword again, but I didn't need to give it any power, even though I thought it felt a little less charged than the last time.

However much was left, it was still more than enough to use in combat if a shadow catcher arrived and I had to deal with it. I gripped it and made sure I had a decent distance between Neritas and me.

Being careful, I slowly tapped the edge of the shield

with the blade. The shield held, and Neritas kept it in place, allowing me to increase the pressure. No matter how much force I put behind it, the shield remained intact and the blade didn't cut through.

I backed off to make sure I didn't notch the blade and powered up the sword a little more. It seemed to draw on just my power, which felt strange and made me wonder exactly what it could do, but now wasn't the time to test it in other ways.

With the sword powered up more, I tried again, but it still didn't cut or damage the shield. It was as if these two things were made of the same metal and as strong as each other, or powered by the same thing.

"Thank the stars for that," Neritas said when I stopped for the second time. "I want something I can trust to hold between me and that sword when you start flinging it around."

"We don't have to do this. I can figure out an alternative if you want," I said as seriously as I could. A part of me wanted to rib him, but I also wanted both him and Flick to know that their safety was important to me.

"I think we all know your training is needed. You'll save my ass at some point in the future and make up for me having to hold this shield now."

Although I hated to admit it, even to myself, Neritas was right. Danger was in my future, especially if I was leaving the city again, and I had no idea what the future would hold if I did prove I was the royal heir that Neritas hoped I was.

I pushed myself to focus and, this time, tried to attack with the blade, fighting and attacking while he dodged around. At the same time, I focused on drawing on my magic, using what was in the weaponry to attack.

I felt invigorated in a way that I normally didn't when fighting, even after several minutes of intensive moving around and attacking. It was almost as if the weapon sustained me too, and I could have kept fighting.

As the fight continued, I noticed Neritas growing sluggish. I pushed him as far as I dared before I grew worried that I might hurt him simply because he was tired.

When I stepped back, I saw that Capricia had come down off the bridge and was watching more closely.

"You need more training from a professional. All of you."

"You offering?" Neritas replied without missing a beat.

Capricia tilted her head to the side for a second before nodding. Without me giving consent or having a chance to express an opinion, Neritas stepped aside for the city guard, and I was suddenly facing a new opponent.

Hoping this was a good idea, I watched as Neritas handed her the fancy shield. I didn't like her holding it, and a part of me wanted to snatch it back, but I reminded myself that she was trying to help, and so far, she'd proved her worth. If she was going to take it or expose us, she'd have done it already.

"Okay, let me see what you've got." She met my gaze and changed her stance as if she was preparing to defend herself.

I attacked, doing my best this time and not holding back. As I'd have expected, she blocked me easily with the shield and every strike I made for the next couple of minutes.

I knew she would be harder to work against. She thrust back with the shield and dodged, almost treating me as she would a shadow catcher. It made me move faster, but again, I could draw on the energy in the sword as well as use it to keep it charged.

"Enough," Capricia said after about five minutes of sparring.

I didn't feel like I'd achieved much, but I had the consolation of seeing how much more out of breath she was and how it had drained her more than it had me. Was this because I could draw on the energy in the sword and make it more efficient?

Almost immediately, my mind jumped to how it had felt to pull on the energy of other people to fuel myself. Had I been doing that without realizing? I didn't think I had been pulling it from the people, but from the sword.

"Is everything okay?" Neritas asked, making me realize I was staring at the sword with a disgusted look on my face.

I nodded, hiding my fears and feelings.

"This is all really strange." I tried to give them something and stop them from staring at me. "I don't know how it all works yet."

"It clearly gives you advantages. You're not even slightly tired after all that. We're fighting on sand with a weapon you're not familiar with, and you're not even sweating, despite your bad technique." Capricia shook her head, staring at me and the sword with wide eyes.

Her point only made me more worried. I had been using the power in the sword for my benefit, and that meant I had been using their power for my benefit, even though they had given it yesterday when I had filled the sword up.

"I think it's the magic in the weapon," I said, tentative and flicking my gaze between their faces to gauge their reactions.

"It helps you?"

"Yes. I think so. I'm using the power we all put in to somehow make my body...stronger."

"That's so cool," Flick declared. "Turns out red dragons get the best power after all."

I blinked, not sure how to process his enthusiasm for it.

"You don't seem to like it. Does it hurt?" Neritas asked, coming a little closer again.

Shaking my head, I tried to think of how to describe it.

"With the sword, I don't even realize I'm doing it." Our eyes met, and I saw him frown briefly, but he nodded as if whatever thought he'd had was gone now or had been pushed away.

"Let's carry on training then. If you can get better at fighting, you can be even more efficient." Neritas focused on Capricia as if he was giving instruction.

Grateful that it took the spotlight off me trying to explain, I listened to Capricia and tried to follow her advice. Eventually, the sword ran out of charge, and the lights on it went out.

"At least it's nice and clear when that thing runs out," Flick said.

"What does it need to power up?" the guard asked.

Neritas and Flick both stepped closer and put their hands on my shoulder, not needing me to answer.

"It comes from us," Neritas replied. She looked at each of us, not quite understanding.

Guilt swept through me, combined with a strange eagerness. I wanted to do this, and at the same time, I didn't. None of them hesitated, however. Capricia put her hand on my shoulder once it was explained to her.

I hesitated anyway and had to push myself to focus on the task. Slowly I connected to all of them, their magic ready and easily accessible to me. Although I tried to be careful, the sword seemed to want to be filled, and it felt natural to keep up a steady stream of power flowing from all four of us.

Although I could have carried on, I stopped pulling on everyone else and added in a bit more of just mine again. It was a strange feeling, but I supposed the others appreciated it.

We went back to practicing shortly after, and I gave Flick and Neritas a turn each, noticing that they could use the sword and it was more effective for them too, but they couldn't draw on the magic inside it the way I could. It gave me a chance to get used to handling the shield and gave Capricia a break at the same time.

By the time both my friends had taken turns attacking me, we were all worn out and ready to stop for the evening. The sword made the use of the magic more efficient, and the charge held in both the blade and the shield until we were done.

Once again, Capricia brought the bridge up after us, although there were no shadow catchers today. We left her there, checking to make sure nothing came to the city in pursuit of me again. I wanted to reassure her that they wouldn't appear if they hadn't already, but I knew it was better to be careful than not.

When I got back to Ben's, my friends quickly said goodbye and left me. I found Ben sitting at his desk again. He smiled when he saw me and held up another letter.

"That was fast." I sat in the nearest chair.

"Yeah, he must have replied to the letter we sent right away."

It took all my self-control not to demand to read the letter or snatch it out of his hands, but I waited patiently for him to let me know what it said.

"He's invited us to meet him and to provide what we need and discuss everything. Even expressed excitement about the idea of meeting you."

That made me pause and frown. Given how many times the shadow catchers had shown up when I did and having already been betrayed by at least one person I thought was an allied dragon, I was wary of this enthusiasm.

"This is the guy giving you money every month, Scarlet." He took my hand. "If he was going to betray you, he could have done so many times already. If this man didn't want what was best for you, he wouldn't have been providing for you so much of your life."

"What if it's not him?" I asked, letting out yet another paranoid worry that had occurred to me.

"It's always possible, but I believe this is the right man, and we will be cautious. I will be with you every step of the way, and we can take your fancy new sword and shield."

I nodded, more than a little grateful that he was taking me seriously, even for a fear that I knew was probably unfounded. He was doing everything he could to stand by me and reassure me. With any luck, he would be proved right and not me.

"There's more," Ben said a moment later.

"More?"

"Yes, he's mentioned knowing where your mother is."

I couldn't move. My body was fixed to the seat as I tried to digest the information. My mother? She was alive?

A cough came from one side of us, making us both jump. Neritas stood near the door.

"Sorry, I tried to knock, but there was no answer, and I panicked when I heard the talking and it sounded intense." Neritas shifted slightly, looking more than a little uncomfortable.

I'd never seen him that way before. It was almost sweet.

"It's okay. I'd rather know you care enough about keeping Scarlet safe to barge through a door between you than not. Especially given everything going on."

"She's royalty, and almost no one knows. Someone has to start making sure we don't lose our last chance at a queen."

"But if my mother is alive, I'm not. She is, surely?"

Ben shook his head, and Neritas sat on the end of the sofa. "Not necessarily. Your father is likely to be where your royal blood came from, but there's only one way to find out."

"You should go meet her if you can. See if you can persuade her to come back here or something." Neritas folded his arms.

"We were discussing that," I explained. "It is going to be dangerous."

"Everything is dangerous. This is a chance to get more

information and meet some family. It's worth it no matter how dangerous it is."

I looked between the two men in front of me and knew there was no other sentiment. This was my chance to gain a family member and answers. If anyone knew what happened to my past and why, my mother would know.

Eventually, I nodded. "Okay. I'll go meet her and this benefactor of mine."

"Then it's settled. I'll find a way to get the elders to let us leave once again." Ben smiled and sat back.

No doubt he would come up with something, but it remained to be seen if they would accept it or not.

CHAPTER EIGHT

Breakfast sat in front of me, and I couldn't touch a single bit of it. Ben had tried to make pancakes for me to get me to eat, but I felt too sick.

"Are you sure about this?" I asked Ben for what must have been the third time. I didn't want to allow the elders to question me again. It felt like a trap.

"If we're going to leave the city, this is the only way. Will you trust me?"

I sighed and nodded. Of course, I trusted Ben, and I needed his guidance. There was still so much of the city and its unspoken rules I didn't know or understand. I had no hope of navigating it successfully alone.

When Ben realized that I wasn't going to eat anything either way, we gave up on breakfast and left his apartment. Once again, my usual companions fell in beside me, Neritas giving me an understanding nod and Flick wearing his usual grin.

To my surprise, Capricia was also with them, and she gave me a nod.

"The elders wanted me to make sure you all got where you needed to go safely and that everyone was okay with what's happening today." It was a strange request, and it made us all pause. Ben frowned, but he didn't say anything, and he squeezed my hand as I opened my mouth to question her. I saw him shake his head the tiniest amount and had to swallow my questions.

This didn't look good. Though Capricia said it was for our safety, I got the feeling the guard escort was nonnegotiable. The elders were insisting on us coming before them like prisoners, under armed guard. The only thing missing was a set of shackles.

Ben had said it was necessary to see them and that he hoped they wouldn't ask too many questions because we wouldn't be able to lie without them knowing or at least picking up on it not being entirely truthful.

It wasn't the first time I had needed to speak in front of them, but that didn't make me any more eager to do so. I wanted to run from the city and go somewhere neither the dragons nor the shadow catchers could find me. But I also wanted to follow this lead.

I'd barely slept all night, wondering what it would be like to meet my own mother for the first time. I had so many questions for her and for my benefactor, and I had imagined both meetings in so many ways. Did she know I was alive?

With Capricia and Ben on either side of me, I drew more attention than ever as we made our way up to the elders' council area. I was pretty sure that the entire city knew we were being seen by the time we got there.

A lot of dragons flew overhead in circles or around the

nearby towers, performing circular routes that gave them the best view. Some of them were more surreptitious, but not many.

Neritas and Flick kept close by my side, and Ben also kept his eye out for dangers as he led the way. It was something I'd gotten used to, and it felt as if I might need it today.

We got to the tower unscathed, however, and everyone kept their distance. Maybe the elders had known what they were doing when they had sent Capricia to escort us.

Ben had reassured me that I wouldn't have to say a lot and the focus would be on him. Although I was an adult in the human culture, I wasn't an adult in the dragon culture, and he was responsible for me in lieu of my actual parents. He could speak for me, but I had no doubt that I would be asked at least a few questions.

The guards outside the elders' chamber parted for us immediately. Capricia seemed to open the door with her mere presence. We were held in a small antechamber for a couple of minutes, and then we were invited into the main chamber in front of the elders.

All of them were sitting at various seats around the far side of the room, the curve of the tower wall at their back giving them a natural semi-circle setup around their audience. It was as intimidating now as it had been the first time.

Ben bowed, and so did everyone else, so I quickly followed suit, hoping that no one particularly paid attention to my delay. As we straightened, I met the eyes of one of the men, and he gave me a gentle nod.

It helped me feel a little calmer. Some of them had

seemed brusque in the past, and to have a warm or friendly gesture reassured me that they weren't there only to judge me but also to hear what mattered.

"Thank you for seeing us on such short notice. I know that everything regarding me and Scarlet has been less than regular already, but I hope you can understand my desire to take Scarlet out of the city once again."

"Irregular would be an understatement," Brenta replied. She didn't sound happy about it, but she was the elder I liked least. The last time we had returned from our trip outside the city, she had come to greet us and asked several questions. Thankfully, they had been outside the chamber, but I was sure the elders were still trying to find out what I'd been up to and shed suspicion on my actions.

"While I understand that things have been difficult for both of you and that settling into a city such as this after living in the human world for so long must be difficult for Scarlet, at some point, this does need to stop, and all ties to the outside world need to be severed, or Scarlet needs to leave and make her peace with never coming back." Another of the elders leaned forward to say this, his glasses almost falling off the end of his nose as he did.

I was pretty sure it was a not-so-veiled shove to do the latter, but Ben only smiled politely as if he hadn't caught the hint.

"I know that you prefer a dragon to be committed one way or another, and I agree that it's important not to divide loyalties. This city is my home, and I hope it will be Scarlet's for her lifetime as well. But her past is even more complicated than when we take an illegal dragon in, and on top of that, her color plays an important part." Ben spoke carefully, choosing his words and making sure there was truth in everything he was saying.

"Scarlet's color is why we have already given so much leeway." Brenta continued to frown.

"I have every reason to believe her mother, another red dragon, has been discovered."

There were gasps at his words, and several of the elders shifted. He had their attention far more than before. None of them spoke, giving him the chance to continue to make his case.

"When I volunteered to speak for Scarlet as a dragon of another color, I was told that it was a temporary measure. That you would all have preferred it if she had a dragon of her own kind to guide her. I think that might be possible, but they want to meet Scarlet, and they're scared. You all know the shadow catchers are more active lately, for some reason or another."

"That does seem to be the truth," the kinder gentleman replied.

I looked at them, still trying to figure out if this was good news to them or bad. Some of them appeared excited, but I had the impression that Brenta was suspicious and perhaps unhappy about hearing that another red dragon was alive in the world. Everyone else was too difficult to read.

"What do you say to all this danger?" another one of them asked me.

"There's danger in everything for me, it seems. And I have a chance to find out who my mother is and where I've truly come from. I've been alone a lot of my life and now have been given the chance to find family. I will be as careful as I can, but unless you plan to imprison me, I'm going to find my mother. Anyone would." I looked the questioner in the eyes, knowing every word I said was entirely truthful.

It was followed by an awkward silence. How could any of them advocate for locking me up rather than letting me go find my mother?

"How confident are you that this information is correct?" Brenta asked, clearly not giving up on trying to stop us.

"As confident as we can be. Or we wouldn't be here," Ben replied, bringing the focus back on him.

Although it seemed as if they had no angle left to argue, I still expected something to be thrown at us. I was sure they wanted to stop us.

"How long do you think this will take? It seems as if Scarlet is missing a lot of her schooling, and she was already so late to begin."

"I've already finished most of my classes or been offered further classes that are non-mandatory in most areas." I didn't enjoy the insinuation that I needed to study more. Other than the history of the dragon world and this city, I was almost done with classes.

"I think I have heard enough. We all know that life has been difficult here for Scarlet. I personally endorse her finding more dragons who would allow her to connect with her heritage on one condition. It should be part of your mission, so to speak, Ben, that you try and encourage her mother to return with Scarlet if possible."

"She may live in another city," Ben pointed out.

"And if she does, then she would be welcome to return

there and offer Scarlet a home with her. But it is always in our nature to ensure that all dragons are given a home if possible, and if we have found that there are more dragons out there who have never lived among us, it would be important to rectify their situation for their safety if nothing else."

"I agree." Ben smiled and bowed. "We should definitely be looking out for the safety of any dragons not protected by another city. I will do my best to help Scarlet's mother as I've done for Scarlet, and make sure she has a home."

It took me a moment to school the features on my face so as not to show the amusement I felt at this evasion. He hadn't promised to bring her back, merely to make sure she was safe, yet he'd said he agreed. He agreed enough.

"I request permission to accompany Ben and Scarlet for the safety of the pair." Capricia stood and stepped forward as she spoke.

Ben's mouth dropped open, and I gulped, but both of us recovered swiftly. This was not what either of us had expected. When Capricia had appeared earlier in the day, I had assumed she was just doing her job, carrying out orders the elders had given her. I hadn't thought she'd be trying to muscle in on our plans. While she had been helping me in one way and kept some elements of what was going on secret, there was far more that I didn't trust her with and wasn't ready to.

"That sounds very wise if you think you can help them stay safe." Brenta smiled, making me like the idea even less, but I couldn't oppose it without arousing suspicion.

"I'm the best person in the city to do so," she replied.

"On the point of safety, I would also wish to go with

Scarlet. I've been helping to keep her safe while she's been in the city, and I'd like to continue doing so." Neritas bowed and stepped forward beside Capricia as if he was signing up with her.

Only a fraction of a second later, Flick also stepped forward and pledged to protect me.

Brenta smiled at both of them. "I have some reticence on more of you going into danger and Capricia having an even harder task, although I commend your bravery and loyalty to your friend. I know you have helped Scarlet become a member of our city. You both have my respect for that."

"These two have actually begun training to aid in guard duties with me, to help them keep Scarlet safe," Capricia explained. "I saw no harm in indulging their desire. Having them with us would aid all of us in being safe. Their experience is broader than it appears."

Brenta nodded in acceptance. "Then I am satisfied as to the dangers to all of you. If you are committed to going as a group and protecting each other, the group of you should go, but I hope that you find everything you're looking for and return soon. With any grace from the stars, we will see six dragons return to us."

This was everything that needed to be said and done, and I felt as if we had gotten off lightly compared to how much we could have been quizzed.

No one said anything but "thank you" as we walked out again and returned to Ben's apartment.

"We need a few hours to gather our stuff and pack up the car. I imagine you want to do the same as well, Capricia?" Ben said when we were at the door of his apartment.

She nodded, glancing between us.

"I'll be ready whenever you all are. Just head to the car."

I tried not to worry about it, knowing she was offering support, but it still bothered me that we might need to be more careful about what we said and did on the road than before. When I had left with just Ben in the past, I had been able to relax. This time I wasn't going to get to do that, and it was going to be more intense than ever.

"We should pack as well, but it won't take either of us long. We'll come back here when we're ready." Neritas flicked his head toward the door and got Flick to go with him.

I didn't go to pack as soon as they were gone. Instead, I sank into a chair and sighed. I'd already put a few things into a bag that morning, intending to leave either way, but now that the meeting was over and I had the permission I needed, I was exhausted. On top of that, I was feeling the transference of my nerves solely onto what it would be like to meet my mother.

"We've got this. I know it's not going to be easy, but whatever happens, you've always got me." Ben sat beside me, not heading to do his packing yet, either.

"Thank you," I replied, not knowing how to voice anything else.

"And I'm pretty sure those two fellas are going to go to the ends of the earth for you if need be."

"Neritas told me he wanted to put me on the throne."

"He wants something to believe in. He wants hope and a reason to fight and get up each day. It might seem scary, but I'm sure if he knew you didn't want something, he wouldn't force it on you. Supporting you is giving him a reason to live."

I frowned, surprised by what Ben had said. My friends had a lot more going on in their lives than I realized, and yet they were focused entirely on me. I needed to change that. They were people too.

CHAPTER NINE

As soon as Flick and Neritas came back, the four of us stood in the living room for a moment.

"This might get dangerous, and there's almost certainly going to be shadow catchers to fight or run away from at some point. If you want to bow out, now is the time."

"We're good. Someone has to go get answers with Scarlet and find out what's actually going on. It can't just be the two of you." Neritas folded his arms, a bag over his shoulder.

"It sounds like you don't entirely trust Capricia." Flick looked between Ben and me as if hoping to read the answer on our faces.

"We don't trust anyone we don't have to, to some degree. Anthony died because of a force we don't understand, and they've been coming after Scarlet ever since. We don't know whom he trusted that betrayed him, but we believe he was betrayed."

"And we've already been betrayed once," I added to

Ben's explanation. "We thought we had a friend, and they turned out to be a handler."

Neritas and Flick both nodded. I'd told them some of this before, but it helped to remind them.

"Then we'll make sure that one of us is always with both of you and work with Capricia only as much as we have to. Let her help us keep you safe but not let her put you in danger if we don't need to."

"I don't want anyone risking their lives. I've got the sword and shield you found me. If we have trouble, I'll focus on getting us out and finding another way to my mother." I set my jaw, determined that no one else would lose their life for me. This was down to me now. I had to make sure that I was the one in danger, not them.

With an understanding of the exact situation and an agreement on how best to handle it, we went to the small section of the city that was attached to land. A small parking lot held Ben's car, along with others.

As we went toward the usual car, Capricia came and stopped us.

"Ben's car isn't going to be large enough for the five of us and everything we'll need. I've opted to take a larger vehicle." She waved us after her and walked over to a large SUV. There was already a fair amount of gear in the back, but we added our stuff along with it.

I noticed there appeared to be camping equipment and a couple of tents. "What is all this?"

"I want to make sure we don't interact with any humans while we're out there."

"None at all? I don't particularly want to camp rough everywhere we go," I replied, looking at Ben.

Capricia came around the SUV to stand right in front of me.

"I don't doubt that you're used to doing this exactly how you please, and I don't want to get in the way of anything safe or necessary, but I've been put in charge of keeping your ass alive during this, and that's what I'm going to do. If that means I have to piss you off by making you sleep in a tent instead of on a feather bed in a hotel, then so be it."

As she stomped off, I set my jaw, not sure what to say. I didn't appreciate being spoken to like I was a spoiled princess, but I hadn't asked for her interference. Ben came up close to me.

"I know she's irritating, but let it go and think of the bigger picture. We'll make it work." Ben gave my hand a quick squeeze and headed to the driver's seat.

Capricia got in his way there too.

"I'm driving us. I want you to be the navigator, and I'll make sure we don't drive into anything dangerous that you might not see."

This was the point I'd have expected Ben to protest, despite what he'd just said to me. It looked as if he considered it, a frown flitting across his face before he gave way and stepped back so Capricia could get into the driver's seat instead.

Ben got into the passenger seat, and that left me in the back with my two companions. Before I knew it, I was sandwiched in the middle and realized I'd been flanked again. It was almost as if the four of them had orchestrated it.

The guards let us straight through, and we were soon

on the road. Almost immediately, Flick pulled some snacks from his bag and passed them around. Since I hadn't eaten breakfast, I was grateful, and it helped break the tension.

I settled back for a long ride. We had to drive for a long time today and even more the following day, and that was to meet our initial contact. We didn't know what was going to happen after that or where we were going to go.

I tried not to think about what was going to be ahead of me. Instead, I talked to my friends. Neither of them had ever left the city before, other than its immediate surroundings, and I quickly realized they had no idea what the human world was like and what was in it. Although I wouldn't have admitted it out loud, I was grateful that Capricia was keeping us away from too many humans.

Even if I wouldn't have been in any danger directly, I suspected Neritas and Flick might draw attention simply by having no idea how to interact in the human world. The dragon city had no stores. No money and no unmet needs. Neither of them had ever had to buy anything.

On top of that, Detaris was built so differently from the average town in the US. They marveled at how spread out the houses were, how much land was around them, and all the cars and busyness everywhere we went.

I tried to explain LA to them. What it had been like working, how money worked, and everything my life had entailed.

"So you have to buy everything you need, and you have to work to get what it all costs?" Flick was more serious than normal.

"Yes, pretty much. We have bills and coins that have

certain values." I reached into my rucksack and pulled out some of the loose cash I had lying around to show him. It boggled his mind, but he looked at it and passed it to Neritas.

I caught Ben glancing back at us, an amused grin on his face, and I wondered if he'd once had a moment like this where another dragon had needed to explain how the human world worked. From the day I had met Ben, he'd appeared comfortable in the human world. I would never have suspected that most dragons never went outside their city.

"I don't understand why you don't all just provide what's needed and go help out where needed. This seems...unnecessary to make sure your needs are met."

"People think this is better, and in some ways, it can be, but it also means that some people go without everything they need."

Flick's mouth fell open as I explained poverty and how people sometimes lacked what they needed. I knew it sounded horrific, and I had to admit it was nice living in the dragon city and not worrying about any of it. But equally, I couldn't imagine the larger world being as easy to provide for in the way that the city did. Could it scale up? I had no idea, but I wasn't about to tackle that problem either.

I tried to explain more, but it was quickly clear that I couldn't do it with words, and it would be something they would have to experience and understand for themselves. Ben rescued the conversation with a suggestion to get lunch and take a break.

Capricia agreed it was a good idea, but instead of pulling into a diner or drive-through, she found a small lane off to the middle of nowhere and pulled over. She grabbed food from the back—pre-packed sandwiches and a picnic lunch.

While I was grateful that she'd thought of providing for us, I lamented the opportunity to show Neritas and Flick what it was like to order food and pay for it and go through a drive-thru or something similar. Though I wouldn't be getting the chance right now, I was determined to give them at least some experience of the human world at some point.

We were only an hour back into driving after lunch when I heard the buzz of a phone in my rucksack. I frowned, confused by the noise and where it had come from, before I realized I had packed the phone that Jace had given me, just in case. She had been an ally against the shadow catchers and had provided backup in the past, so I had told her some basic information about the plan.

Ben had also believed it wise to at least give her some basics, but I hadn't expected to hear from her any time soon. I pulled out the phone but put my finger to my lips while Capricia was distracted by cars on the road so Neritas and Flick wouldn't say anything while I read it or if they saw her message.

It could only be from Jace, and at first, I worried that she might need me or have information that might prove this trip to already be futile. Instead, I found that she had been working on helping us.

My group has questions and I've been asked to bring some extra dragons to ensure your safety in this matter, especially given the shadow catchers that got between us meeting several days ago. I have the information from then and have reached out to your contact as well. I'll meet you there.

I frowned, not sure how to convey this development to Ben or stop this ball from rolling, or if I even should. I reread the message several times, and Neritas and Flick both read it over my shoulder.

"I've got an interesting message," I said a few minutes later. "From our liaison. She says she'll meet us there as well."

Ben turned in his seat and raised his eyebrows. I held up my phone to show him and made sure it was at an angle so Capricia couldn't see.

"Okay, looks good to me. I don't think we should worry about that. She knows what she's doing, and it sounds as if she is safe."

"She usually keeps herself safe," I said, hoping that it appeared innocent enough.

"There's a human? Or a dragon?" Capricia asked, glancing at me in the reflection in the rearview mirror.

"Dragon. Someone Anthony knew." I met her gaze, grateful I wasn't under a spotlight anymore.

"From another city?"

"Possibly. We tried to get her to meet this guy for us, but we didn't think she was going to be able to."

"So you didn't know she was going to be joining us

when we were talking to the elders earlier?" The suspicion in her voice was clear.

"How could we know? She just messaged me. I asked her to help a few days ago but hadn't heard back. I thought she was busy. We tried to get her to do this for us so we didn't need to leave the city."

"And you didn't think to mention that to the elders?"

"No. Like I said, she didn't respond, so she was not even in the picture. And besides, you know this wouldn't be the first secret we've kept." I kept holding her gaze, not liking how shrill she got. It was a reminder that she was already in this situation with us, and I was aware it sounded like a threat, but I couldn't think of an alternative.

Capricia didn't respond, and the car descended into a frosty silence. After this argument, I didn't dare speak for a while or add anything that might cause any more tension. This wasn't the relaxing drive I hoped I'd have for something so important in my life. I was going to meet the person who had been providing for me, and hopefully my mother.

No part of me wanted someone I didn't fully trust there, but now I had Jace and whoever she was bringing as well. Admittedly, she'd probably bring other dragons I had already fought beside, but it was yet more people who would be witnessing something I would rather do solo or just with Ben and my friends.

We continued driving on until several hours after dark, and then Capricia pulled over somewhere remote again. This time she moved to the back of the SUV and started pulling the tents out.

"Grab anything you don't want to leave in the car overnight. We'll be a bit of a walk away from it," she said.

Although I considered protesting, it was likely to be too late now to find somewhere else to stay, and I could tell that there wasn't going to be anywhere comfortable to camp near the SUV. We had little choice but to follow her into the nearby countryside and find somewhere to pitch a couple of tents.

We had a lot to carry when all our camping equipment, food, and belongings were gathered up, but none of us complained as we carried it down a narrow trail. It reminded me a little of the trail I'd gone down with Ben, Jace, and Cios a few weeks earlier.

Although I didn't voice the perceived similarity, I reached out with my mind to feel for anything that might be lurking for us. I knew I wouldn't be able to sleep that night. Unless I had been in my apartment or a few other specific places, I had never been safe from the shadow catchers for long. I didn't expect to be this evening either.

As we trudged on, I wished it had been something that had occurred to me earlier, but I knew a building or a room would make little difference if a shadow catcher got my trail. They could either move straight through physical barriers or they rotted them away. I wasn't sure why they sometimes did one and sometimes another, but I'd seen them do both and had to run many times.

Capricia had only been with me once when I had been struggling against the demons, and she had waded through the middle of a river with me to get ahead of them and have a chance of fleeing.

I was grateful to notice the growing sound of running

water as we followed the trail. It grew louder and louder until we reached the edge of a river. If nothing else, we would at least have a safe place to flee tonight.

Reluctantly appreciating the choice of overnight location, I helped set up one of the tents and tried not to think about how tired I was despite sitting in the car most of the day. With any luck, I'd get a few hours' sleep, but I wasn't going to count on it.

CHAPTER TEN

It was still only a few hours into the night when I gave up trying to sleep and crawled back out of my tent. I had been almost commanded to sleep not long after we'd eaten a basic dinner cooked over a bonfire. I had to share the tent with Capricia, which had been enough to annoy me, but she'd also insisted on taking the first watch.

I tried not to think about how dangerous it was out here and felt for any telltale signs of evil with my mind. There weren't any, but knowing that hadn't made it any easier for me to sleep, and I'd found myself keeping awake to check again and again. I couldn't stop thinking about the last time I'd been out of the city and in the wilderness.

Capricia was standing a little way off from the camp, but to my surprise, Ben was in front of the men's tent, drinking what looked like a beer and sketching in a little book I hadn't seen before. He looked up as I straightened and smiled at me.

"Couldn't sleep either?" he asked in a whisper. I shook my head, my eyes on the back of our guardian.

I couldn't entirely make out whether she'd wanted to come with us or felt it was her duty, and I couldn't decide if it was a blessing or a curse to have her presence.

All I knew for sure was that this hadn't been how I'd imagined this trip to pan out, despite all the ways my brain had attempted to do so. I was grateful when Ben pulled out a candy bar and handed it to me, though. I sank onto the edge of the log he was on and tried to process what I wanted to do next and if there was any point trying to get more sleep or if I should suggest Capricia sleep.

My sword and shield were sitting with my pack inside the tent, but I couldn't be bothered to get back up and go get them. They were safe if nothing else, and if Capricia went inside or I felt danger, I would be sure to get them. Until then, their location didn't matter so much.

I continued to reach out and around me. I had been able to feel evil more intensely and farther out than I'd realized the last time I had tried it. There was still nothing, however.

Eventually, Capricia appeared to notice me and came back toward our camp.

"You should get some sleep," she said, sounding as if it was no hardship for her to take the first watch or possibly stay up all night.

"I'm not sleepy anymore. You get some. It appears as if you're going to insist on driving again." I didn't hide the frustration in my voice. I might appreciate her help, but I also didn't like being told what to do, and this time of night, I wasn't at my best.

At first, she looked as if she was going to object, but instead, she shrugged.

"If you want to be up a while and keep us safe, be my guest. I know that you can do funky magic." Capricia disappeared into the tent but reappeared several seconds later with my special sword and shield. I had been summoning up the motivation to go get them myself, but I thanked her, grateful that she'd done it.

When she didn't say another word but went straight back inside, I guessed that I had also irritated her.

For a few minutes, I sat beside Ben and looked up at the stars. We were far away from any towns, so they were clearly visible. It made me think of the flight lesson a few weeks earlier in the city when I had climbed as high as I possibly could.

The first time I'd tried it, I had pretty much passed out and fallen a long way, but I recovered and was able to make a second attempt. It was one of my favorite moments as a dragon in flying lessons. I loved how it felt to soar so high that the curve of the earth could be seen, and I had to control my breathing so as not to pass out.

I considered it now. Just flying up and so high that I was entirely undetectable. Needing something to take the edge off my nerves and stop my compulsive checking for monsters on top, I whispered my desire to Ben.

"There's a certain delight in being able to run away from it all, isn't there?" he replied. "I wish I could tell you to go ahead. It's one of the best feelings in the world, to fly. But we both know that it's a bannable offense in the city, to fly outside it. We're not allowed to do magic outside a city at all."

"But what happened after I flew in LA? I should have been banned by that logic."

"And if you remember right, I had to advocate for you, and you almost did get banned before ever being admitted into the city. Only being a ward of Anthony's and the first red dragon in the city in some time saved you, I think."

"So don't risk it now because I'm on thin ice?" I asked.

Ben let out a brief chuckle and nodded.

"You know that's not likely to stop me if I need to use magic or transform into a dragon, right?"

"It's not stopped you in the past." Ben looked my way, an amused smile on his face.

He had a point. I'd turned into a dragon and flown over a locked gate in the past, and I used magic every time I killed a shadow catcher. Of course, I'd felt that all of those instances had been necessary for our survival, but I hadn't needed to make my case, thankfully. There had been no human witnesses apart from one small occasion, and they'd been sworn to secrecy.

I didn't expect anyone to believe them either, even if they did talk.

But the more I did magic, and the more I was in dragon form while in the human world, I knew I was increasing the risk that someone who could get the world's attention might notice. I didn't doubt that it could cause a lot of problems if I wasn't careful.

"We wouldn't need to be camping or taking so long if we flew," I added.

"But you'd have to fly slow to give us a chance to keep up with you. Flick says that he's had a moment or two where he's struggled to keep up with you, and no one else beats Flick."

I raised my eyebrows, surprised by this admission, but I

didn't respond. It didn't change the fact that flying wasn't an option. I knew that would be taking it too far.

We fell into a companionable silence as I nibbled on the candy bar and laid the weapon and shield over my lap. Now and then, I checked if demons were nearby again, but we really did appear to be in the middle of nowhere.

I must have dozed in and out a few times because the bonfire's strength kept changing. Ben and then Neritas added fuel to it as it died down, disturbing me when they moved about. Every time they did, I checked for shadow catchers, but it wasn't until the sky started to brighten and the sun threatened to rise that I felt something on the edge of my reach.

"Something is finally nearby. I think it's time we got back on the road," I said when Neritas looked my way.

He got up and went toward the nearest tent to call inside. Before I could do the same to Capricia, she emerged. I reached inside, and we pulled out our kit and quickly stuffed our sleeping bags back into the sacks they'd come from. I marveled at how swiftly everything packed back up again and we could get it back into a pile.

Neritas and Flick put the fire out as Ben and Capricia picked everything up.

By the time I'd got my pack and pulled out my shield and sword, I didn't have any more capacity to take anything else, and that meant the others had to carry more, but I didn't argue with anyone as Neritas, Ben, and Flick split my packs between them instead.

"To the river?" Ben asked me as Capricia headed in that direction.

"No. The car. For now, they feel as if they're on the other side of the river and away from the car."

I didn't elaborate or explain that I could also feel a presence on the other side of the road, beyond the car. It was different and the only one not moving closer. Whatever it was, I was sure I could at least handle having to possibly kill one of the demons. I had an almost perfect combination of companions to draw magic from if nothing else.

We moved as a tight-knit group, the trail nice and easy to follow in the growing light and a path opening out ahead. I still clutched the sword and shield. Both were charged up a little, and that meant I was already ready for battle.

The uneasy feeling in my head slowly grew, but it was still behind and back toward the camp we'd occupied. I had detected it with enough time to get us out of there before we were trapped between several shadow catchers at once, multiple coming in from different directions instead of following our trail as they had in the past.

I was grateful for the early warning system I had as we hurried along, and I picked up the pace, jogging and considering whatever it was that was less distinct ahead of us. It was also moving, but not as fast or as predictably, and that had me more concerned than the stronger uneasy feeling behind us.

Despite all this going through my head, I kept silent, and no one else in my group spoke either. It was better that we got back to the car as swiftly as we could and didn't hang around. I wasn't going to be able to fight all of them at once, and I didn't want to try.

When I saw the SUV, the relief was immediate. We all

naturally sped up a little, Neritas coming up the quickest and popping the back so we could load everything.

I quickly chucked my bag in and turned to face the incoming danger with my shield over all of us while the rest of my group packed up the car. Before he got in the car, I noticed Flick grab the bag of food and pull out some breakfast bars and snacks so we could eat on the go, and then Neritas and I were the only people not in the vehicle.

He stood by the open door, waiting for me as I backed up, still unable to see the shadow catchers but knowing they were on the way. I hurried to his side, clutching the shield and sword, and I tried to look for the other source of discomfort in my mind.

It was strange, and I was sure that it was nearby. Looking over Neritas' shoulder to the other side of the road, I thought I saw something moving, the flash of what looked like a person as they moved from behind one tree to behind another.

"What?" Neritas asked. He shifted to look that way too.

"I'm not sure," I replied, trying to remember what it had felt like to notice the handler. When I'd first met Fintar, he had seemed like a normal person, and I wasn't sure if this felt the way he had when he'd revealed himself. I hadn't felt that enough times to have any confidence in it.

Either way, I had the presence of shadow catchers getting closer from behind us, and I didn't want to delay us when we had an easy way out today. I hurried into the car, handing the shield to Flick and putting the sword down on the armrest toward the front of the car so I could strap in. I took them back as Neritas followed me into the car.

Capricia pulled away to get us out of there and back on

a decent road. For a few minutes longer, I felt tense and closed my eyes, trying to feel the demons nearby and work out what they were up to and if they knew they had lost their quarry.

We were soon too far away for me to properly feel them, but I was fairly sure that the handler had been there and that he had come across the road not long after we left, joining his minions. I shuddered, thinking about how close we had come to danger yet again. It really did follow me everywhere I went. What I didn't understand was how.

How could they work out where I was going? Was there a tracker, something that marked me out? Could they feel me the way I did them?

I'd asked some of these questions before, but I never seemed to get any answers. I was always left to wonder and know that something was happening but have no idea what.

A part of me wanted to suspect everyone. To go off alone and see if it put me in danger. But there were others I cared about, and I had to know they were safe before I could walk away from them, even if one of them might be a rogue and feeding information to the handler somehow.

Now I had the sword and shield, and I could actually test a few things, knowing that I would have something to draw on. Until I'd used it in combat, though, I had no idea if that was wise. For now, I would have to wait and hope that it all became clear soon.

And if I didn't get answers from the people I met, I knew I wasn't going back to the city this time. Unless I had what I wanted, I was going to keep looking, Capricia and her job be damned. This was my future and my destiny, and I was done letting other people decide how it played out.

CHAPTER ELEVEN

It wasn't long before lunch when my stomach rumbled. All the snacks were gone. None of our meals had been as plentiful as those in the city, and unlike when I traveled with Ben, there had been no stopping for anything but gas, and even then, we'd been instructed to stay in the car.

Although that had still been something fascinating for Neritas and Flick to observe, it wasn't the same as being able to walk them through the whole process and buy them something of their own.

"I think we're being followed," Capricia said, breaking the silence.

"Followed?" I turned in my seat to look behind. I hadn't felt the presence of anything dangerous, but a car followed fairly close behind us on what was an otherwise quiet road.

I looked at it a few times, and then it clicked. I had seen the car outside the restaurant in LA a few times.

"Slow down a little, so they get a bit closer," I said, hoping Capricia wouldn't argue.

Thankfully, she didn't, choosing to trust me.

"It's Jace," I said a few seconds later, recognizing her distinctive hair and face in the passenger seat and the tall figure of Cios behind the wheel. I waved and grinned, trying to get their attention.

"Jace?" Capricia asked.

"Yes, the person who said they'd meet us and bring some more backup. Good dragon. One of Anthony's friends and someone we can trust. She's saved my life already."

It didn't take them long to recognize me, and they waved back.

"Great. So we're now a convoy." Capricia sighed but said no more.

She didn't need to. The temperature seemed to drop a degree or two, and any jovial chatter we might have been able to draw out of her through the journey was gone. Although it made the atmosphere worse, part of me found it funny.

She had invited herself along on my mission and made it less than what I wanted it to be, and I had to get over that and work with it. Having Jace join us and put Capricia out made me feel as if I had gotten a modicum of revenge. The feeling was a little petty, and I knew it, but I didn't feel much guilt. I hadn't planned it. It was, as they say, karma.

I kept an eye on the car behind us, using the rearview mirror to look over my shoulder without having to turn. More than a few times, I met Capricia's gaze as she did the same, but we both acted as if we hadn't noticed it.

By the time my stomach was feeling empty, we had reached another town, and the looming welcome sign of a drive-through made me want to suggest we use it. We had more food in the back, and I knew we could easily eat that, but Cios signaled to turn in, and I took the opportunity to try to get this whole trip to go more the way I wanted. It was still petty, but I also wanted to find out what Jace knew and if she had some idea of what my sword and shield could do.

"Go with them," I told Capricia.

"We're not interacting with humans," she replied.

Once more, our eyes met, and I saw hers widen a tiny amount. She was afraid. Suddenly it made more sense. Capricia was supposed to be in charge, and she was scared of messing up. Her pride couldn't handle admitting that there were potential threats that she couldn't anticipate.

Instead of facing that fear, she had opted to prevent it from being a problem.

I reached forward. "Please. I need to talk to her and find out what she knows before we get there. We don't have to interact a lot with humans this way, but we can't entirely avoid them for so many days on end. It's just not possible."

I thought Capricia was going to stick to her guns and refuse to pull over, but eventually, she flicked the turn signal on and took us into the drive-through parking lot.

We led the way to the back corner of the parking lot, and Cios pulled up beside us. I decided to leave my shield and sword in the SUV for now and encouraged Neritas to get out so I could too. I had some introductions to make.

There were a couple more dragons in the back of their car. I recognized them from our previous encounter with demons. A young woman and another guy with an almost-shaved head. They'd also both been at the farmhouse afterward and seen their leader acknowledge me as someone important. Merrik also sat with them, a welcome surprise. He'd guarded the gate and been one of the first to acknowledge my gifts with magic.

It made for a warm reunion as Jace walked up to me and gave me a hug. She eyed up the party I had with me—only Ben was familiar to her. At least, I thought only Ben was. When she and Capricia looked at each other, I saw recognition in their eyes, and both of them frowned.

"Still on city guard duty, then, Capricia." The frosty edge to Jace's voice reminded me a little of the first time I had met the dragon. She hadn't liked me much to start with either, and it had taken her a while to thaw.

"Guard captain now, actually." Capricia leaned against the closed driver's door and folded her arms across her chest, revealing the insignia on the uniform she wore.

"You always were ambitious."

"And you always had a strange sense of loyalty."

"I'm not blind." Jace gave Capricia a strained smile that didn't come up to her eyes, and I knew it was time to steer this conversation somewhere else before these two women were at each other's throats.

I quickly introduced my other two new companions to Jace and Cios and made it clear I didn't know the other dragons' names, but Jace introduced them as Tim and Harriet. I thought they might be fake names, especially with the way they appeared to hesitate over responding to being introduced. But I wasn't going to push for real names if they didn't want to give them.

It did the trick, however. The ice was broken by the time we were done. Ben took over, being polite, asking them how they were doing and making small talk. It gave me a moment to wave Jace over to the back of the truck and show her the sword and the shield. Neritas and Flick never left my side, continuing their bodyguard roles even though we weren't in the city, and they were unlikely to recognize a threat of human nature.

"Neritas found these. They seem to store my magical energy once I've combined it and allow me to draw on it later."

"They're charged?" she asked, reaching out tentatively to touch the shield.

Nodding, I showed her what I knew about it and how it lit up, and Neritas explained a little about where he found it. They were talking about that when Capricia came to me and requested that I talk to her.

I followed her, leaving the sword and shield with Neritas so I didn't have them out in the open where I might scare or pique the interest of humans.

"Are you sure about this? I know you have had a different introduction to our world, and Anthony has done some strange things with you, but if you knew where these dragons came from—"

"I do know," I replied quietly, meeting Capricia's gaze. "They're not quite what the dragons in the city think they are, but even if they were, *they're* the ones out here helping me and keeping everyone safe. The shadow catchers are more active for a reason, and the elders are in denial. I know you care about protecting people. Right now, they're on our side."

Capricia studied my face.

"You really trust them?"

"To help us in this? Yes, just as I trust you to do what's needed to protect other dragons. It's in your nature and theirs to be who you are. No one is all bad, and no one is all good. They want to help us, and they seek the same answers."

"Okay, then I will follow your lead and protect you. Because one thing is for sure. You're special, and whoever your parents are, they were important."

"I'm getting that impression." I sighed.

She gave me a wan smile before we rejoined the group. From then on, Capricia was warmer, and we soon stowed the artifacts back in the SUV where they wouldn't be seen.

"Let's all get some lunch and figure out this last part of the journey and how we want to start this meeting," Jace said, clearly also used to calling the shots.

For now, I let it go, took the arm of each of my favorite companions, and went toward the nearby fast-food place. A part of me was excited about showing them what it was like in the human world and how I was going to pay using a small piece of plastic with a chip in it.

It was fun to watch them look around, but they had the sense to keep their interest and awe muted, so no one stared at us beyond the first glance of noticing a large group of adults arriving.

Ben went first, followed by Jace and her group, and they set the standard of what to do and how to be natural. It gave me time to explain the menu in whispers to Flick, Neritas, and Capricia, proving my hunch to be true—she had never done this before, either.

As soon as it was my turn, I ordered confidently and stepped aside for the others. Neritas ordered as if he'd been doing it for years, and Flick was almost the same, tripping up on the drink and needing me to point him toward something he liked.

Capricia hesitated, and her order came out in a rush, which meant she had to repeat the last half of it. Once she was done and I'd paid, there was a hiccup, however. The dragons were baffled by the next part of the process, but they didn't say anything until we were off to one side and waiting for our food. We whiled the time away waiting for the food by my explaining what had happened.

Their eyes lit up when they were handed trays piled high with food. I'd encouraged them to order well, since it wasn't expensive, and these three had sizable appetites. My own tray left no doubt that I was equally hungry today. It was a strange thing, but I had missed the substandard and almost crappy burgers served in a place like this.

One of the other orphans I had grown up with had refused to ever eat fast food, saying it had no place in civilized society, but part of me loved these crazy places. Something about them was comforting. We didn't get to go to drive-throughs often, but they always went along with days out.

So many memories were attached to these things, and the nostalgia was what made them worth it. Not the quality.

We took a large table out of the way and squeezed ourselves around it, several of us eating off the trays on our laps. Neritas and Flick practically inhaled the food, confirming I wasn't the only one who hadn't thought much of Capricia's camping food supplies.

By the time we were finishing up, Jace had a map open

on her phone and was showing us the derelict industrial area where our contact had asked us to meet him. Now that I saw it, I wasn't sure I wanted to go there and meet anyone. How could that be a good place to meet?

It looked like the perfect place to be ambushed by shadow catchers or Fintar, and I told them as much, but we all realized we had no choice.

"Since there's more of us, I recommend that we take a two-pronged approach and that Scarlet shouldn't head into the area until we know it's safe." Jace looked at Ben, Capricia, and Neritas, and I knew that she'd already got the measure of those who held the most power in the group or played protective roles.

It was strange in some ways but smart of her as well. I wanted to push back, knowing I was also their best protection, but there was another flaw in her plan that would sell my desire to be closer better than anything.

"I can feel them. When they're nearby. I know roughly where they are, how many, and I'm beginning to get an idea of what a handler feels like when they're controlling shadow catchers too."

Jace sighed and nodded.

"Despite that, we need to keep you safe."

"We'll bring her in closer but not so close that we can't get her out of there," Capricia provided the middle ground for me and gave me a nod at the same time.

I continued to relax a little more, grateful. It looked as if my team was going to work together, all of them putting their egos aside to do what was needed.

I wasn't the only one who wanted answers. Although I didn't know Tim or Harriet's stories, I knew everyone else here was invested in one way or another. They either wanted to know what or who I was, or they had another reason to pursue this route to the end. We were all in this together, even if I was the one who held all the puzzle pieces.

CHAPTER TWELVE

The last half hour of the journey was the worst as the tension continued to grow. My phone sat on top of the shield on my lap. The sword was beside it, making the strangest picture when considered as a whole. If I had been dressed in medieval garb or going to a renaissance fair, my lap full of objects might not seem so strange, but in a car full of normally dressed people, this was out of place.

Yet everyone was acting as if they were normal.

My phone displayed the map and the route to our destination. The sound was on, and a strange female voice read the directions to Capricia. Once we got to our waiting point, I was going to concentrate, see what I could feel, and then figure out if the rest of the plan was safe or not.

If I hadn't been nervous about that and how many more people would be in danger along with me this time, I'd have been nervous about whom I was meeting. And I was anxious about both. I just had one hurdle to tackle before the other.

The time passed, and the distance to go got shorter

until Capricia was pulling up outside an abandoned factory of some kind in an out-of-the-way parking lot. I tried to focus immediately, closing my eyes to get the best idea I could.

Although it *felt* safe, I wasn't sure it was. I was so anxious that I'd lost confidence in my ability to pick up on threats at the edge of my reach.

"Deep, slow breaths. You've done this lots of times before. It's no different today," Ben said, his head turned toward me.

He had a point. I shouldn't find this part difficult. Feeling out threats was almost second nature to me by now. I knew where they were instinctively.

I took another couple of breaths and focused. Having Ben's words echo around my head helped me to feel outward, and I could pick up on the strange feeling on the edge of my mind.

"There's a handler, but he's not close. I don't think he's a danger as long as we don't linger."

"Get Jace to head in, then, but give her the heads-up. If it stays that way, I'll take you closer as well." Capricia set her jaw, making it clear that she didn't plan on being argued with regarding this failsafe.

I tapped away on the extra phone Jace had given me and waited for her feedback. If I'd thought I felt nervous before, this was a whole new level of not okay. Having others go into danger for me and not facing danger myself was so counterintuitive to me that I could barely sit still.

"How's the danger level looking now?" Capricia asked.

"Still the same," I replied, quicker and snappier than I'd intended to be.

She frowned but nodded. "Okay, let's head in, but I want to be kept up to date with any changes, and if I don't like it, I think we should pull out."

"Understood." I shoved the phone in my pocket and grabbed the rest of my equipment as we all piled out of the SUV again.

I led the way toward the rendezvous point. I could just about see the building we were meant to meet in. Jace was approaching from the opposite side. As I got closer, I made sure I was still listening for the possibility of company from other sources, but the strange feeling that it might be a handler remained on the edge of my senses.

Although I knew I could push it out a little and might be able to get a better idea, I was too divided right now. I needed to know what was ahead, and I wanted to meet this person, the benefactor who might be able to lead me to my mother.

None of us spoke. I wasn't sure what to say. They all knew how big this was for me, how important. If this went as well as I hoped, I was going to be meeting my mother soon. Despite having enough realism and sense to know that meeting parents and finding them lovely was a pipe dream for most orphans, it hadn't stopped me from dreaming about it now and then.

I walked closer, ensuring that I was connected to the weaponry mentally as well. It made my mind a little sharper as we reached the outside of the large warehouse.

Pausing, Ben reached out a hand for me and the others to slow. I stopped, wondering what could have him spooked.

"I don't like this. This is a very enclosed space. Is there even another route in and out of here?"

His caution was understandable, but it didn't help me get my answers. I needed to go inside, no matter how bad it was.

I reached out my hand to pull the door open, but it was already ever so slightly ajar, and as I got closer, I realized that I could feel something inside, something dark and evil.

"Pull back," I said as the door burst open toward me. "It's some kind of trap."

Yells and shouts from the other side of the building confirmed that Jace had run into similar trouble, and that divided me.

I raised the shield and took a step back, and my friends pulled in close to my sides.

As a shadow catcher barreled past and through the door, it caught on the large metal object I carried and shrieked. It made me falter, thrown off balance by the force of the collision.

Flick and Neritas braced me between them, and Capricia brought her shield around to one side of me to help protect Ben as well. Without thinking, I sucked on the power of all four of my companions and charged her shield.

With my previous experience and the extra training I'd had, my body took over, and I lunged at the demon before it could fully recover. My sword pierced its side, and another pained cry filled the evening air.

This made it shudder, and unlike previous attacks, my sword left what looked like a tear in its flesh when I pulled back. Normally my attacks made the creatures yowl and pull back, but there would be no sign of a wound. This time was different.

Emboldened, I attacked with a flurry of thrusts accompanied by blocks with the shield. It not only drove the shadow catcher back, but it continued to injure the creature in this strange new way.

Another shadow catcher came out, and the whole door was rotting off its hinges as Capricia blocked the beak of the nearest demon. It made her shield smoke until I charged it again and stabbed the engaged enemy once more.

This strike seemed to do deeper damage, and it puffed out of existence. It made far less noise, almost as if the fight took it by surprise this time or it hadn't processed the danger it was in.

Either way, I didn't have much time to think about it. The next creature came at me, and for a few seconds, we danced with it while I tried to get some advantage. It was more wary, more intelligent again, confirming my thought that a handler was nearby and in control.

"Capricia, swap shields," I called. I lunged at the shadow catcher, pushed it back, and then pushed as much energy into the shield I carried as possible.

She looked at me like I'd grown three heads, but another yelp from the other side of the building made her understand.

"Protect them, please." I gave her my shield and took hers before the shadow catcher in front of us could recover. We almost weren't swift enough, but I caught the next attack with the edge of the weaker shield and charged it again from the magic my companions and I could combine.

It wasn't ideal to only have one of the two artifacts, but it meant Capricia could fall back.

Without looking back, she sprinted around the side of the building, heading toward the second group. It gave me some hope, and they would equally feel encouraged by my sending someone who could defend them, but more shadow catchers were coming my way.

I killed another, but I felt the presence of several coming across the inside of the warehouse and the handler coming closer too.

He was behind me, so I did as I had done in my previous encounter and turned toward him.

"Keep up with me," I commanded as I started to sprint. They did, although I feared I would soon lose them.

Guided only by my mind, I ran toward an office building that stood alone in the nearby industrial lot. Somewhere in the building was the handler. Hopefully it was Fintar, or we had a bigger problem. I didn't want to have attracted the attention of multiple handlers and multiple sets of shadow catchers.

Not that I was entirely sure how it worked and what was truly happening to the shadow catchers I vaporized. I only assumed they were dead. I couldn't be sure they were gone completely. They might return at some point. I couldn't tell any of them apart.

All these thoughts ran through my head, helping me ignore the aches and pains growing in my legs, the lactic acid build-up, and the background fear and pressure in my head.

The shadow catchers in the warehouse were almost entirely following my group—only one stayed engaged with the others—and it meant I was running the risk of getting caught between the handler and his minions. I had to have faith that I could do this. The power in the sword I now wielded was different from the one I had imbued in the weapons I wielded before.

It wasn't decaying, and I had the three best dragons with me. If Capricia and Jace had any sense, they'd come after me with their group and bring us all together. That was something I couldn't sense, however. I had to trust and hope they knew what they were doing.

As soon as I got close to the offices, I felt the handler move. My group was running fast and hard, and I barely slowed when I reached the door, barreling into it with a charged shield between me and it. The door splintered and gave inwards, almost pitching me onto the floor as it jarred the side of my body.

I was going to feel it for some time, but I was determined to make this handler regret his choices, so I carried on as best I could. I was feeling the sprint, but I could also sense him trying to get out of the building. He was upstairs and moving to the back of the building.

"Up?" I asked the companions with me, noticing that they were panting but still with me, and all had determined expressions.

We spread out, each of us taking a different route off the foyer we were in. I only found a bathroom and a dead end, but Ben called for me.

"This way."

We converged on his spot, and I went ahead once more.

Taking the steps two at a time, I focused on the connection I had with my companions and drew on their powers the tiniest amount before combining the magic.

Not sure if it would help or not, I fed it back toward them, giving them mine and trying to fuel them the way I had fueled myself. It seemed to help. All of us perked up, and I felt my aches fade into the background a little more.

When we were on the correct floor, I looked for the best route toward the handler. Where he had been standing, I saw a strange black sludge on the window and floor, and the smell of mold and fungus made me wrinkle up my nose.

I only paused for a second before I carried on. The strange feeling in my head pinpointed where he'd gone. I used the charged shield to touch the door on the far side of the room and push it open, heading into a large, empty, open-plan office. A splotchy trail of something dark and slimy led to the far door, and I ran beside it.

The handler was on the other side of it—I felt him, but I could also feel the shadow catchers getting close to this building. I hesitated for the first time, aware we might get trapped if I wasn't careful.

"It's over," I called, deciding to bluff as I often did when I had no idea what else to do. I could handle him, if nothing else. "Come out of there before I come in without what little mercy I am feeling right now."

As I yelled, I heard the pounding of more footsteps behind us, signaling that Capricia and the rest of my companions had joined us. She still held the shield, but it was no longer lit up, and Harriet had a wound on her shoulder that made it obvious she had been hit by a shadow catcher.

I waved them all over, and we swapped shields.

"Last chance," I called again as we finished and she slipped back.

I connected to all of the dragons, and I felt them activate their powers. Whoever was on the other side of the door was going to be faced with a group of pissed-off dragons.

There was a laugh, and I felt the shadow catchers come into the building.

"Keep an eye on the rear," I said to Capricia and hurried forward.

Although I was moving slower, I tried the same approach as I had with the building entrance and ran at it with the shield braced against my shoulder.

I heard the crackle of electricity and felt heat come off it when I hit, followed by the crunching sound of wood giving somewhere. It held enough that I didn't manage to break all the way through. I pulled back as Capricia yelled something I couldn't hear over the din, and I hit the door again.

It gave the second time around, and I rushed into the room to see another empty office fit for a single manager. The slightly shadowy figure of the handler was breaking his way through the wall on the far side of the building.

The handler fell to the ground, the evening light causing his partial shadow body to look eerie. I paused for a second.

"Red, we need you," Jace called from behind me. I whirled to see Capricia trying to take the hits from two shadow catchers while another came crawling up the now rotting stairs.

Everywhere, I could smell the pungent, accelerated decaying of the building itself, and I knew this was going to get dangerous.

"Try and get down, out that way," I said to Ben as I ran past him to help Capricia and Jace. Cios held a shield, too—a pleasant surprise—but it was already partially ruined.

Yelling and making enough noise to wake the dead, I commanded everyone to get behind me and close their eyes.

Before I could be sure they'd heard me, I lit myself up like a Christmas tree, flashing brightly for a fraction of a second. It stunned the shadow catchers in place and allowed me and the others time to recover.

They got behind me, Cios and Capricia bringing their shields over to either side of me as I thrust at the nearest shadow catcher. Trying to remember what Capricia had begun teaching me, I hacked and slashed and drew on the dragons' magic to make my body move and everyone around me feel more invigorated.

With such a large group of dragons to draw on, I soon vaporized another shadow catcher, and the two remaining demons hesitated, their movements more sluggish.

"Time to go," Ben yelled, sounding slightly muffled, from behind.

We continued to fall back but didn't turn our backs on the creatures. The floor began to sag toward them, and we backed up faster until we reached the doorway.

"Get out of here," I told my two closest companions. Everyone else was already in the office behind me.

Not sure if it would help or not, I grabbed the broken door and tried to shove it back into place. It didn't quite fit, but it was a barrier of sorts that would buy us a little time while Capricia and Cios eased themselves out of the broken section of wall and down to the ground where everyone else was waiting to help them.

I made sure I was last, and before I finally turned and almost threw myself at Neritas and Ben, a shadow catcher was partway through the door, their body somehow morphing through it.

Keeping the sword angled out and away from everyone, I made an ungraceful descent and hurried away from the offices after the entire group. Jace and her team had already run toward their vehicle, and Capricia was encouraging Flick back to ours.

"Let's get out of here," I added. Neritas and Ben, reluctant to leave me, had waited.

It was all the signal they needed, and the three of us sprinted hard for the SUV.

Thankfully, we'd doubled back when we had run from the warehouse to the office block, and it gave us less distance to cover to get to safety.

Once again, I dove into the back of a car as Capricia screeched away.

We left behind two shadow catchers and a handler I could no longer feel. All of me hurt and was exhausted.

CHAPTER THIRTEEN

Tumbling back out of the car, I hurried over to everyone huddling together and immediately harnessed the magic in the sword and shield and fed it back to my dragon companions. Jace was looking over the wound on Harriet's arm.

"It doesn't hurt," she said.

"That thing should. It should look worse than it does too." Jace frowned and pulled out a first-aid kit anyway.

As I moved closer and tried to get a better look, Harriet smiled at me.

"I think someone's magic has helped in some way. It hasn't hurt since we rejoined Scarlet."

I grinned, grateful to hear something I was doing was making a difference.

"What the hell was all that?" Capricia asked, slamming her shield down on the ground nearby.

It was moldy, broken, and not going to hold up much more. Cios brought his shield out of the car and placed it beside hers. It didn't look much better. My shield and sword, on the other hand, were fine and still covered in a pattern of glowing lines.

"A handler and his shadow catchers," I replied when I realized the city guard captain was staring at me as if she expected me to have an answer. I didn't. Not really.

Everywhere I went, I had to face things like that. And it was tough, but I didn't have much choice about it. She had signed on to help me. Had she expected anything less than that level of danger?

"That was a trap, pure and simple. And you ran headlong into it."

"I was pretty sure that I almost got to a handler, actually. If I'd been a little bit quicker in—"

"We were all caught in a building with shadow catchers after several of us had already had to fend them off without enough support. And there was no sign of your contact."

"There was." Jace turned to Capricia. "I caught sight of someone else fleeing before we hit the first shadow catcher. And I know this might be hard for you city dwellers to handle, but this is what it's like out here in the human world right now."

"What do you mean?" Capricia turned an even darker shade of red, and I thought she might explode with anger.

"Fighting shadow catchers is a way of life for us. We have no way of hiding from them the way dragons in the cities do."

"It's not my fault that you—"

"Enough!" I yelled, getting between them before either of them could take another step toward each other or magic could start flying. This wasn't what needed to happen.

Both of them looked at me as if they were going to argue, and I worried that I had done nothing but stir up a hornet's nest and make the problem worse. As I looked between them, Jace started to relax, and it gave Capricia little choice but to try to do the same.

"Okay. If our contact showed up and then fled, we need to find him again as soon as possible. He could be in danger."

"No." Capricia took another step toward me. "I'm taking you right back to the city."

"No. You're not. You can drive back there if you don't want to help me anymore, but a man who has been providing for me for years is possibly in danger because he dared to finally meet me. And on top of that, he knows my mother. I will find him if I can."

Capricia gritted her teeth and clenched both fists, but she didn't argue with me.

Eventually, I looked away from her studying gaze and back to Jace.

"You said you had spoken to him as well. We have an address for him, but it's not necessarily a good way to find him."

Jace tilted her head to the side. "Leave it with me. Rest up for a short while. Let's all get some more food and recover. I'll see if a contact nearby can get us any more shields, and then we'll try again."

With nothing else to do but what was suggested, I nodded and focused back on Harriet. Neritas was already pulling food from the SUV and sharing it out. Capricia looked as if she might also object to this, no doubt because it was meant to last us the journey home, but whether the food would last without us needing to hit a store was the least of my worries.

I tried to help Harriet more, pulling on our combined magic and focusing on her wound, but nothing happened except that she said she felt stronger in general. By the time I gave up, Neritas and Flick were back by my side with sandwiches in their hands and trying to encourage me to eat.

"You need to eat and recover as well. We need your magic if we're to face all this." Neritas pointed to the nearby parking lot wall I could perch on.

He had a point, so I let him take care of me for a moment and went to sit down. Ben joined us and munched with us.

"Did the sword do damage differently? Did I see that right?" Ben asked when we were all finishing up.

"I think so." I explained the difference as far as I could tell, grateful that I wasn't the only one who had noticed that it appeared to actually physically wound them, unlike my previous weaponry.

"And it didn't decay like the shields and the wooden sticks you used on the beach," Neritas pointed out.

That was another good observation. Something about these items made me think they had deliberately been designed to fight shadow catchers. And if they had been in the city, it meant that someone at some point had decided that the knowledge of how to defeat them should be taken away from everyone.

I feared what that meant for my future. I hoped that whoever they were, they were long dead, and the elders in charge were now entirely unaware that it was possible, but a part of me wanted them to still be alive. I wanted them to be held accountable for Anthony's dying. If he had known he could defend himself, that there were tools he could have used, maybe he would still be alive.

I exhaled, shaking my head. Tears threatened to fall.

Neritas put his arm around me, and Ben shifted closer and took my hand.

"We'll get through this. We don't have to fight again today or find this contact if you're not ready." Ben's voice was gentle, the concern clear.

"It's not that. It's the city. I got used to fighting the shadow catchers. I worry about all of you, but it's knowing that these weapons could have helped Anthony. If Anthony had brought me to the city sooner, I might have been able to keep him alive."

"And if you had come to the city sooner, something else might have killed him or you. He kept you away for a reason, and we have no way of knowing what would have happened. I know it's easy to feel as if it is your fault or wish you could have done something differently or better, but the choices were made with the best knowledge we had at the time. That's all any of us can do."

I tried to smile, but I wasn't sure it came across. Slowly I calmed down, already thinking back to today's battle.

"What was that thing in the office?" Flick asked a few minutes later, his mind on the same event. "It looked like it might be human, but it was the same sort of creepy shadow as the catchers and decayed and rotted whatever it touched like they do."

"A handler."

"Do you think it was Fintar?" Ben asked.

"You've seen this handler before?" Neritas let out a low whistle and ran his hand through his hair.

"I think so. Yes. He's been the threat all along, I think. I'm pretty sure he killed Anthony. He approached us in human form the same day we met Jace for the first time. And he spoke of Anthony and me as if he knew about both of us. Made me think he was another person that Anthony had trusted."

"Sounds like Anthony may have trusted him. You definitely can't blame yourself for his death."

I shrugged, surprised by how calm my companions were. I'd dragged them into hell to fight its minions and drawn more than a little magic from them during the fight.

"I'd understand if either of you wanted to go back to the city now," I blurted as I looked at them.

Neritas shook his head, and Flick vehemently said no.

"This is crazy, don't get me wrong. And scary. I'm not as stoic as Neritas." Flick nodded at his counterpart with respect. "But I'm seeing this through. In the city, the best I can aim for is showing off at flying and honing my skills even further, for no other purpose than to say I can. Here I can make a difference. I helped you kill several shadow catchers today. I helped kill a demon."

"We all did." Ben grinned, and even Neritas looked a little brighter and raised his chin a fraction higher.

"It makes the world safer—everyone in it. It's a purpose that almost no dragon in the city has. It might be dangerous, but I could die knowing I've made a difference now. That my life meant something other than vanity and sports."

"I'd prefer it if none of us died," Jace said, interrupting as she returned.

I looked up at her, giving her my undivided attention.

"We've managed to get a message to this guy of yours. He's willing to try again and has given us a new location. He said he would be there in four hours."

"Four hours?" I asked. It was already dark, and four hours from now was going to be a very unsociable time.

"Sounds like he wants some sleep first. We should probably do the same."

"Possibly. He said he won't get there first this time and won't turn up if he's not satisfied that it's safe for him. I think we should all get a quick nap and then head in early." Jace didn't take her eyes off me, and I picked up on what she wasn't saying. She wanted me to fight and kill any shadow catchers there before he could be spooked away.

"I'm going to need to rest between now and then. As much as possible. You should all rest as much as you can. Or at least the strongest dragon we have of each color." It was a cold statement to make, but this was also part of my strategy. The truth was that I needed certain individuals more than others when it came to dealing with the enemy.

"You took the words right out of my mouth, Red. Consider it done. Go curl up in a car along with the team you want, and we'll get the two least needed to drive us around for a bit and make sure nothing can sneak up on us."

Grateful that Jace had gone further in her planning already, I finished off the last few bites of cake I'd been munching on and downed some water. It wasn't ideal, and I would probably be hungry again when I awoke, but at worst, I could persuade whoever my driver was to head to a drive-through for wake-up time if I needed to.

Capricia almost growled when Jace told her to relinquish her keys and let Harriet drive our SUV.

"I need you to be rested, too," I told her.

"But I won't be able to sleep in the car with you. You won't be protected."

"We'll have Harriet follow Cios. Capricia, you can sleep right alongside me." Jace acted like this would settle it, but Capricia didn't trust her either. It was a lot to ask of her.

"I'm not going to let anything happen to Scarlet," Ben said, stepping in near Capricia before I could. "You're one of the few people who knows what Anthony meant. Who could have some idea of why I have done everything I have done. If you can't trust anything else, trust that. Trust what you know of my heart."

Although he was vague and spoke quietly so the entire group wouldn't hear his words, this did have an impact.

"I don't like it." Capricia held out the keys to Harriet.

"You and me both, sister. Have you tried to drive with a shadow catcher wound? I want to be asleep, I assure you."

It was a good point, and it made me wince and turn to her.

"Don't start being concerned for me," she added, raising her chin and puffing out her chest a little. "I'm with everyone else on this. I saw you cut one of those monsters to ribbons earlier. I'm good with this war wound. I've got one of the best stories ever to go with it."

I blinked as she grinned, and for a second, I wondered if I simply had some of the most insane people as companions. Either way, we had all come this far, and I wasn't giving up now.

Hoping my trust wasn't misplaced, I got back into the SUV and tried to work out how the three of us could sleep in the backseats. It wasn't going to be easy, and Ben offered me the passenger seat when he saw us struggling, but in the end, I opted to cozy up with Flick and Neritas.

They had been my friends for long enough that it was only awkward at first, but something about knowing we were buddies in everything and we would do whatever was needed for each other made it okay. In the end, Neritas hugged me while I hugged Flick, and we used sweatshirts and a blanket to prop Neritas in a good position.

I caught a grin on Ben's face before he settled down for sleep.

Not uttering a word to disturb us, Harriet pulled out, taking us off into the night on a tour of the area that we wouldn't see.

CHAPTER FOURTEEN

A gentle hand woke me up, and Neritas and Flick also stirred. Our bodies were even more of a tangle of limbs than when we'd fallen asleep.

"Okay, that's going to be a way of sleeping I'm not sure I'll want to repeat." Neritas winced as he shifted.

"Sorry," I replied, thinking I didn't feel too rough for the unusual sleep position and instantly being hit with a good dose of guilt for it.

"It's okay. When all this is done and dusted, I can tell people that I have been a royal pillow and aided the dragon queen in her slumber." Neritas grinned, and I was pretty sure I heard Ben chuckle, though I couldn't see him well enough in the dark to tell.

"If you were a royal pillow, what does that make me? The royal teddy bear?" Flick asked.

Now everyone did laugh, including me. The mental image they'd both painted was exactly the light relief we all needed.

"We're about to arrive at an all-night fast-food place,

and then we'll head out again. Got to keep the troops fed," Harriet explained.

It felt good to think Jace or someone else had anticipated my every thought. It was beginning to feel like we could handle this, and I might get used to being in this role if it stuck.

As we collected our food from the drive-through window and pulled into a quiet part of the parking lot again, I noticed Capricia had only just woken up. I'd expected her to get antsy about us interacting with humans again and eating junk food, but she took her food and joined in the outside picnic.

I let everyone eat in silence for a bit before I encouraged Jace to pull up a map of where we were meeting. It was another out-of-the-way area, this time an old treatment plant and a dried-up section of what had once been a diverted river. Even less chance we would bump into random humans, especially at this time of night.

While I looked at the map, I tried to work out where the best places to fight shadow catchers would be, where to park, and what sort of careful sweep we might want to make. It would help that I would be able to sense the danger, but it would also help if we could use the land and area to our advantage.

Fighting shadow catchers one by one was a lot easier than facing down two at once. And I wasn't splitting the group this time. We didn't have the extra shields. Even if Jace could get new ones, it wouldn't be for a day or two, and we needed them now.

I encouraged them all to head there as soon as we could, and many of us took our food back into the cars.

The sooner I got there, the sooner I could deal with a threat and hope I wouldn't have to run away. It wasn't far away from where we were—Harriet and Jace having planned our pit stop well.

As we got closer, I felt the familiar tightening of my spine and sweaty palms that accompanied my anxiety. Though the weapons I had made it easier to fight the shadow catchers, the monsters weren't nothing, and they could do some damage. I'd been lucky so far. One day that luck might run out.

We drove in silence, with nothing to stop me from brooding or running frenzied possible scenarios through my head.

Sitting in the middle of the car gave me the advantage of being able to see the satnav Capricia was following. The city captain was back where she felt she ought to be, in the driver's seat. Jace was in the car behind us, understanding that it was safer to let me lead when I could sense the danger, and Capricia would have advance warning if we needed to abort or take a different direction.

So far, I couldn't feel any danger, but I didn't think we'd get away with none at all. I was almost certain that we would have to kill a few more shadow catchers before the night was through. Thankfully, we were all as rested as we could be under the circumstances.

As we got closer to our destination, Capricia slowed. The road became less even and more unkempt. It was clear it hadn't been used in a while, and the once pristine tarmac of the road was lost to creeping plants and moss, and it was no longer two cars wide.

I still couldn't feel any evil, so I urged her onward until

we were close to the spot we'd picked out to park. A staff parking lot had once been here, and it meant we could move into a larger open area. Only as we were pulling in did I feel the faint sign of something that might be trouble.

It was clear that we weren't going to be alone for long, but I couldn't work out the exact level of the threat we would face. That was going to take some time to become clear. Knowing that evil lurked here already made me more sure that either someone was helping this handler or I was drawing him to me by accident somehow.

As we all got out and gathered around, I focused as much on what I felt coming as on the people around me.

"I think we should leave a driver each with the cars," Jace said before I could begin strategizing.

"It would need to be the same drivers as earlier," I replied. I didn't like the idea of leaving the two most sleep-deprived dragons by themselves.

"I could stay with them," Tim offered. "I'm the only other color double up, and my shield is still relatively intact. It could keep us alive long enough to get to you or flee. You're not going to be far away if you're hunting these things."

It was a good point, but it worried me. Only when I noticed the look that passed between him and Harriet did I make my mind up. They were sweet on each other, and he wanted to protect her.

"Okay, that's what we'll do. If you can, keep the cars running, but above all, keep yourselves alive. Call Jace if you need anyone, and be prepared for trouble if I'm nearby or not." It was the best advice I could give. They'd faced shadow catchers before. I got the feeling that everyone who worked with Jace had some idea of how to handle the monsters, even if only a few of them had managed to fight back in any way.

By the time everyone else had formed a group around and behind me, with Jace and Capricia holding large hunks of wood instead of shields this time, I could feel what I needed to.

I could sense a handler, and I hoped it was Fintar, but he wouldn't be my target this time, although I intended to make it look like it at first. On top of that, it felt like at least three shadow catchers. They were coming in from several directions, but not all at once, which was what made me hesitant to declare that there were only three.

Each pinprick of unease on my mind could represent more than one monster at that distance. It was too difficult to tell when they were still so far away.

With Jace holding the map to let me get a rough idea of where the handler might be, I started us off in that direction. At first, this appeared to make no difference to the movements of any of the demons. They continued in the direction they had been going, heading toward the abandoned parking lot where we had left the vehicles.

It made me want to turn around and go back to defend the three we'd left behind, but I knew that would put us in the center of what the handler thought was a trap. I couldn't do that. I had to be smarter.

Instead, I picked the uneasy feeling of a shadow catcher closest to the handler. I made my way toward both the handler and the monster, closing the distance between my prey and my decoy prey and increasing the distance between our group and the cars.

I had to hope that I could draw the attention of the beasts soon enough to keep the three people we'd left with the vehicles safe. There was a good chance that the handler would bring them toward my position if he thought I was a threat to him. It would make it harder to pick the shadow catchers off one by one, but it should keep my friends safe.

When I was getting close to a shadow catcher but still couldn't see it, I put my finger to my lips and lowered the light from my shield and sword a little more to make sure it wasn't lighting us up like beacons and was just enough to ensure we could see without tripping over our own feet.

With an entire set of colored dragons with me, I had already connected to their power, now able to do so before they'd touched me as long as they were all close enough. I didn't know if it was a skill I was learning, or if it was easier to connect to people I'd figured out before, or if more time with a person made it easier, or some other theory, but it was useful.

None of them needed to rest a hand on my shoulders anymore, and I was sure they could feel that. None of them needed to be told when I could connect to them or not. I was grateful for the heightened intuitiveness. It made my task easier.

If I was going to power up the gate meant to contain the greatest demon of all, having dragons who were used to this around me was a good start.

Now I had a shadow catcher to deal with, however. Despite my intention of sneaking around, when I saw this one, I picked up the pace and headed right for it. It was uncharacteristic of any dragon in the last few hundred years, it seemed, but I attacked it before it could register that I was close, and I stabbed into it with the charged sword.

It let out a shriek I was growing used to, making me wonder if I could find a way to shut them up with the first attack, though it never seemed to kill them. As its beak hit the shield, I felt it reel in pain, and I grinned.

With a full team, I could really damage these things.

Although it was dark and I couldn't see the creature as well as I would have liked to fight it, Capricia's training was already paying off, and it took less than a minute for me to kill this shadow catcher. It became a cloud of smoke that drifted away on the breeze.

That left only two of them, and they were both behind me.

"Nice work, Red," Jace said. No one had come close to being attacked or hurt this time.

"There's still two more, at least, and the handler yet. How long have we got until our contact is meant to show?" I asked.

"About an hour. But I'm pretty sure if he turned up and saw you doing that, he wouldn't run away again."

She had a point, and it made me feel a little better about the likelihood of this plan working. All I had to do was get to the third one before he showed up.

I closed my eyes and checked what I could sense. The handler had changed position, coming closer while I'd fought, but he'd also moved off to one side as if he was trying to get behind one of the remaining shadow catchers.

It gave me some hope that I had definitely been killing these monsters. The handler could normally call in more and more of these creatures, but it seemed like he was running out.

Taking off again, I headed toward him and the shadow catcher he was trying to use as a shield. He was playing right into my hands, and I wasn't going to complain about such good fortune.

It took another fifteen minutes of trekking through undergrowth and wild terrain to get close to the next creature. Once again, I attacked it before it could notice my presence. This time I aimed for the neck but came in from the side and tried to swing down.

My blow cut downward, but the beast jerked away, and though I'd partially severed the neck, it seemed to be able to function and move as if I had stabbed it anywhere else. The shriek it gave was almost deafening again, and I winced. Next time I went hunting these things, I was going to make sure that I had some earplugs.

I killed it in three good stabs and a couple of smacks with the shield and stood panting, my heart racing. The shield and sword were still well-charged, and I felt relatively good magic-wise, but my body was tired. Not enough sleep and a lot of moving around and chasing down enemies was tough.

Briefly, I considered drawing on the dragons to take away my tiredness, but I knew I wouldn't be able to forgive myself for taking energy I didn't absolutely need, so I carried on, leading them toward the third shadow catcher.

With all three traveling toward me the whole time, this one was the quickest to find. It noticed me at about the same time I noticed it, almost as if the handler was getting better at figuring out where I was or observing through their senses.

Either way, I managed to block its attack and rebuff it. It hit a tree, and the smell of rotting bark and wood filled my nostrils a second later. The pungent smell was tough to tolerate, but the distraction of an enraged monster trying to tear me apart helped.

I stabbed at it, but this one moved faster and with a skill they didn't normally possess, dodging and weaving in an almost human-like manner. The handler was putting everything he could into this attack and making sure it was reacting and fighting with all the wisdom the handler had.

As it dodged one of my favorite attacks, I wondered if Fintar was learning my fighting style from controlling the demons as they fought me. If so, I had to eventually deal with him, or he would become an enemy who one day would beat me on skill alone. Unless there was armor to match the shield.

No sooner had this thought crossed my mind than I almost got hit, only just dodging a beak strike that came around the side of the shield. Concentrating, I moved faster and decided to draw a little more on the magic of my companions.

After easing the aches, pains, and fatigue of walking so far after so little sleep, my mind perked up, and I could move faster again. This was the advantage I needed, and I quickly got in a hit that continued to turn the tide.

With my friends cheering me on, I slaughtered the creature and sent it into dust, or back where it had come from. I didn't much care which.

I felt for the handler, wanting to catch him as well, but

he'd been smart and used the battle as a distraction while he fled. Already he was barely at the edge of my mind, and his presence in my senses was swiftly growing fainter.

As I checked that my companions were all okay, he faded from my mind completely.

Satisfied that the area was now safe for a meeting, I let Jace use her phone to lead us back to the vehicles. I'd gotten turned around in the dark with all the fights and would have led us in entirely the wrong direction had she not thought to make sure her phone knew where we were.

By the time we got back, it was close to the rendezvous time. The three friends we'd left behind were pleased to see us.

I encouraged everyone to rest and waited on the edge of the SUV, sitting underneath the open liftgate and munching on the last of the food.

Thankfully, it didn't take long for another car to pull into the parking lot. It was a sleek sports car, and I didn't doubt that it could move fast, but it didn't look as if it would have fared well on the last mile or so of the road here. I stood to move away from the SUV and turned toward the newcomer.

A guy got out. He looked to be in his late forties, but dragons were deceptive in human form. His hair was dark brown and short at the sides, slightly tousled. He looked tired, his shoulders slumped, and bags hung heavy around his eyes. He kept close to the car and held out his hand to get me to stop as I tried to approach him.

His eyes roved over the weapon I still had slung at my waist and the shield I carried.

"That's close enough. I don't want to take any unnecessary risks. How do I know you are who you say you are?" he asked. His gaze went to the array of companions behind me, where all of them had assembled between the two vehicles we had arrived in.

I tilted my head to the side, thinking of the best way to prove to him that I was relatively safe.

I morphed part of my body while also making the shield shine brighter and lighting me up. I illuminated my red scales in a way that made them shine and almost sparkle.

He nodded almost immediately.

"Forgive my doubt, Scarlet. I have waited a long time to meet you, and I'm honored to finally get the chance."

I exhaled and moved closer, eager to have so many questions answered but also disappointed that he was alone.

CHAPTER FIFTEEN

Once again, we were sitting at a diner. This time it was for breakfast, and I only had some of the group around me. The others were getting some sleep. I'd been sitting in a booth with Ben, Jace, Capricia, Neritas, Flick, and our new contact, Reijo, for several hours while the bacon, pancakes, maple syrup, and coffee kept coming.

"I really can't get over how much like her you look. I should have recognized you right away."

"It's okay, Reijo. I can understand the desire to be careful," I replied. I'd had to reassure him several times already.

Although I was pleased to meet him, and he had confirmed that he was the person paying my trust fund and had been looking out for me for a while, that was about all the substance he had given me. He didn't have proof or evidence with him that I could use. And my mother was nowhere close.

"I'm sorry that I can't be more help," he said, also not for the first time.

So far, we'd discussed why he was helping me, his belief

that he was called to bring dragons into the light and support them in exploring the human world and living in it, and how we had led the shadow catchers to his house and trashed it between us. His knowledge of the house made me trust him a little more.

It was still difficult to know what to do next, however.

"It's really important to me that I find some kind of proof of my birth, and I would love to meet my mother." I hoped that this would help focus him again. It was getting frustrating, I had finished eating, and I was ready to get on with what I needed to do next.

Knowing he didn't have much for me but was confirming some of what I already knew was a strange, bittersweet discovery after fighting so hard to get to this point. On top of that, we'd been bogged down by Reijo's questions about Anthony and everything that had happened over the last few months.

"Your mother is somewhere safe. I can take you to her, but only if we can be sure we're not putting her in danger. She's not at her best, and she has asked me to be careful." His gaze flicked to the group around me, and I frowned.

"These are all people I trust," I said without thinking, hoping I'd picked up on his reluctance correctly.

"Should you?" he shot back. "No offense meant to any of you, but the handler and shadow catchers keep turning up. Sounds like you've got a mole to me."

"It's possibly true, but I've also wondered if they can sense me somehow. I can sense them, and they pop up no matter who knows where I am." It was the truth, but it didn't mean someone wasn't spying on me or tracking me or giving away my plans.

"I know it's tough, but you're asking me to take a big risk on a pretty young red dragon."

"If I remember right, it's me who just took the risk. I killed more shadow catchers in the last twenty-four hours than anyone has killed in years."

He blinked as if he'd not heard me right.

"At least, we're pretty sure she killed them. It definitely seemed like it." Ben shrugged.

For a moment, no one spoke or moved. This wasn't going to plan, and I was tired of it.

"Look. You know my mother. I know you do. You know you do. I want to meet my mother and figure out how the hell to protect this world from whatever is dangerous. You don't need to trust me. You need to trust her. If you trust her, then take me to her and let her make up her mind about what she wants to do with me."

Reijo looked at me and still didn't appear to know how to react, but eventually, he nodded.

"You have a point, but it's not that simple."

"I'm not sure we should be rushing into the middle of wherever this guy suggests," Capricia interjected. "We've been attacked by shadow catchers everywhere we went, and we're out of food."

"So we get some more supplies. Jace picks up some more of the shields and spears that they use, and I'll charge them all up. Even the ones that aren't fancy like mine are good for one charge."

Capricia opened her mouth to object, but Jace nodded and pulled out her phone to make it happen.

I looked back at Reijo, expecting him to pitch in information or help with the plan.

"Well, I guess you're in charge for now. But I warn you. Your mother is a typical red dragon as well."

"Then you're used to dealing with us and know that when our minds are made up about something, nothing is going to change them. Also, if I am who you say I am, then I'm at least a princess or something, so I think I get to pull rank on this one."

Another brief silence followed my entitled rant, and I thought I was going to be told to shut up. Instead, everyone nodded.

"I'll go with Capricia to get food for all of us and load up the SUV," Ben said. "We'll meet you back here in about an hour."

"I'm not leaving her." Capricia almost growled the words.

"We'll stay with her," Neritas replied and shuffled slightly closer to me. I felt Flick move in tighter, too. "You told the elders that we had come along to be your eyes and ears when you couldn't be. We need to split into three groups for a moment, and this is the best way to do so."

Everyone knew Neritas had spoken the truth.

"I'll leave Cios with you as well," Jace added. "That gives you the strongest group you can have in one car while I go get Harriet medical treatment and pick up what we can."

I nodded, knowing there wasn't a better option, but not happy that we had to split up for a bit.

"What are we going to do?" Reijo asked me.

"Let my mother know we'll be joining her, plan a route, and try not to get detected by shadow catchers so they can't follow us. And deal with any that try to get close."

I didn't know how likely we were to have trouble with

any of them. After vaporizing so many, I hoped that there weren't many left nearby, but I had no way of knowing what sort of numbers we'd be fighting against. The last twenty-four hours could be giving me a false sense of security. And it also appeared that Reijo knew very little about the monsters. He hadn't reacted the way I'd have expected to the knowledge that I had hurt some of the demons or possibly killed them. He had been as shocked as anyone else.

Did that mean my mother had never killed any? Was that why she was in hiding? I had a feeling that I was about to find out the answer to that question and many more.

As everyone else left, I pulled out my phone and asked Reijo to let me know where I was going. Again, he hesitated to tell me.

"Do I really have to get angry about this? I want to know where my mother is, and you're the only person who can tell me. Are you going to let me know where to go, or are you going to keep running the risk that the information you know will die with you and the entire world might perish because of it?"

I knew I was laying the guilt on a bit strong, but I didn't care. This was going to happen. I was sick of relying on other people to get where I wanted to go or meet the people I wanted to meet. I was in charge now, and so far, for the most part, everyone was fine with that.

"Okay, I'll give you the village we need to get to, and we can work out the best route to go so that we're less likely to bring trouble to your mother. Sienna, by the way. Her name is Sienna."

I exhaled and nodded, grateful for that information and

feeling some of the tension leave my body. Finally, we were getting somewhere.

He put the location into the map for me and talked about the roads in. It was another three hours away, but given how far we'd come, that was nothing. The only problem was working out how much distance the detours we needed to take would add to the journey.

As soon as we'd identified the best route, I looked for a stopping point a little way away from the village. Somewhere out in the country where I could work out if we had been followed or not and deal with any threats before I brought them to my mother's door. It was clear she had been hiding, and I didn't want to put her in danger.

Of everything I had done or suggested, this thawed Reijo the most. He grew far more cooperative after that. Neritas, Flick, and Cios helped me plan and also made sure they had the route in their phones in case something happened to any one of us and others needed to get where they were going.

I appreciated the support, and by the time the hour we had was up, we had some strategies, Reijo had paid the diner bill, and we were back out by the car, waiting for the others to return and for the next part of my mission to begin.

While waiting, I felt for more threats, but nothing weighed on my mind. Reijo became an asset here, walking me through a technique for feeling them more easily.

"Your mother says that it helps to imagine them, imagine the handler you want to check for, and to reach into the magic within you at the same time."

The last part had never occurred to me to consider. I

picked up the sword, knowing it currently had the stored magic of every type of dragon. It could provide any type of magical energy I wanted if I could make sure I knew how to wield it properly.

With Reijo's guidance, I concentrated and reached out with my mind farther than ever before. I was determined to make us safe and was grateful to find that, for now, we were in the clear. Nothing was close enough to threaten us.

I was letting go and bringing myself back to the normal world when Ben and Capricia returned with the large SUV laden with more food than I'd ever seen.

I wondered if we'd need it, but I wasn't going to put down Capricia's attempt to take care of me when she felt out of her depth. This wasn't what she'd expected. I was sure she thought the trip would be far less eventful. She'd probably thought I wouldn't succeed.

We swapped information, mostly me telling her our plan. She added the route to her phone and urged me to get back in the SUV, but I shook my head.

"I need to ride with Reijo this time. Keep Ben safe for me." I met Capricia's gaze without flinching.

To my surprise, she nodded. "Ben said that you'd tell me something like that. I want to keep you safe. I want to see this through as well."

"I know. And I couldn't have got this far without you. Don't think I don't appreciate you. But I'm the one the shadow catchers are after, and Reijo is the one with the info I need. It's best if I'm with what I need to protect most and away from anyone I don't have to put in danger."

She had no argument for that logic. I considered commanding Neritas and Flick to go with her, but we all knew that I needed their power. Three dragons of different colors seemed to be the minimum I needed to actually kill a shadow catcher. I had to have them with me, and I had to be careful.

Jace wasn't far behind Capricia, but she did hand out what she'd picked up. She had a shield for everyone, and I charged each of them up, drawing on the magic of the entire group. Harriet looked far better with her wound properly dressed, and Tim was carrying a spear. He had three more—one each for Capricia, Jace, and Neritas. I charged those, too.

It added a weapon to each vehicle—always useful.

"Only use these if you have to," I instructed as I gave them to the designated wielders. "They'll hurt the shadow catchers, but alone, they're not enough to kill. And there's a good chance you'll do more to piss the vile things off instead of making things better for yourselves."

They all nodded and did their best to look responsible.

With nothing else to do to prepare for what would come next and no better way to protect us from being followed by demons, I got into Reijo's sleek car. The seats were a smooth leather that I could sink into, and I sat in the passenger seat, grateful to be in the front this time. Neritas and Flick joined us in the back.

Once again, I had my fancy sword and shield balanced on my lap. Reijo glanced at them a couple of times.

"I must admit, there's a part of me glad I've got you wielding those things with me. Your mother has something similar. I've only ever seen her use them once, but it was the most spectacular thing I've ever seen."

"Let's hope you don't have to witness it again, but I'll do my best to be just as impressive if needed."

Reijo chuckled as he pulled away.

I clutched the underside of the shield, grateful it covered my tight grip and the nerves I felt. I was finally on my way to meet my mother.

CHAPTER SIXTEEN

The three hours flew by in a great conversation about how Reijo had built up his finances and how long he'd known my mother. I still got the impression that he was holding back a little, but also that he cared about her and, by extension, me. She had set up the fund for me and implored him to make sure I was okay.

It made me feel a little better about being left alone in the orphan system, but I would have some tough questions for my mother about why she hadn't kept me with her. Living on the state hadn't been easy. I'd not found my happy family or been in homes I loved. They hadn't been as bad as some, but I'd had no loving parents who took her place.

Anthony had been the closest thing to family, and now Ben. And whatever reason my mother had, there was going to be an argument that I'd still have been better off with her, especially now that I knew she was alive.

I wrestled with many thoughts as we got closer, but I also felt gratitude that they had done something to help me. Several times Reijo expressed his hope that the money he'd been sending had made my life easier and that Anthony had been able to help me find my own way in life. I told him about the friends I'd made, the job I'd had, and the day Anthony had gone missing.

Neritas and Flick had never heard half of what I was talking about either, and I knew that it wasn't an easy story to hear, but I told it as best I could. Several times when I was talking about what had happened with Anthony, a lump formed in my throat and I found it hard to talk, but I pushed through.

I would probably have to say it all again when I found my mother, but I said it now anyway. Now was right. Getting Reijo to understand everything I had already fought and what I had faced to be here felt important. I'd told him a little in the diner, but Capricia and Jace had been there, and I hadn't wanted them to hear so much.

Of course, Ben might tell me I shouldn't be saying it now, and I knew I had to be careful about whom I trusted, but this man had been giving me money for years. He had been protecting my mother. He was someone that she trusted. I found it was enough to make me trust him too.

We soon got close to the stopping point I'd requested, and Reijo took a turn into a small parking lot at a park not far from our final destination. As my friends pulled in around us, one vehicle on either side like flanking guards, I closed my eyes and concentrated. I thought of everything Reijo had told me and walked myself through it for a second time.

It was strange at first, supplementing a natural gift with

the magic I carried and could connect to, but my mind was soon sensing a presence in the nearby area.

I gasped as it came to mind. This one didn't fill me with unease. This one came with a strange but much more welcoming feeling. My mother. I knew without it needing to be explained to me. Like a pulsing heartbeat in my mind, I felt her there, not far away. Not long after I sensed her, I could tell she was moving.

"She can feel me. She's coming toward us," I said, knowing that what I could feel, she must as well.

In that moment, I knew everything I needed to know about her. She came to find me the instant she had sensed me. Knowing she was so eager took away most of the nerves I felt.

"Any danger?" Reijo asked, still not pulling away.

"None I can feel," I replied, checking one more time. It wouldn't have been the first time danger had lurked beyond my ability to detect it and then quickly moved in. It made me wonder if the handler could sense me from a far greater distance, but I had no way of knowing if that was how he was managing to track me. And right now, I didn't care. My mother was so close.

Thankfully, this satisfied Reijo. He drove off again, helping to close the gap between my mother and me even faster than she was.

Before long, we were driving down the country lane to her house, a building out alone in the middle of farmland. I smiled when I saw her walking down the road toward us. A smile appeared on her face when she spotted the car.

Reijo pulled over without me asking, and I quickly got

out, shield in hand and sword at my waist. This made her smile grow wider.

"Scarlet?" she asked in a sweet, gentle voice that didn't give any indication of a powerful hotheaded red dragon that might lie underneath the surface.

I nodded.

"My baby," she said as we walked the final few steps toward each other.

"Mom." I didn't know what else to say. All of the words I'd imagined using and emotions I'd thought I'd feel vanished under a combination of fear, curiosity, and relief. This was my mother. The person who had brought me into this world and been through a hell of her own since then.

Slowly she took my hand, her skin the same color and her fingers the same long, slender shape. Her wrinkles and scars were the only indications that she wasn't me, or a sister. We were family. That much was clear.

"I could sense you," I added when my voice decided to work again.

"As I could you. Your mind is already growing powerful. You must have been practicing."

"She's already killed several shadow catchers," Reijo said as he joined us. "At least this lot with her tells me she has. I didn't get to witness it, not that I'm complaining."

Instead of being pleased, my mother frowned. She seemed to notice Flick and Neritas standing farther back, as well as the two other cars behind ours. No one else had gotten out, but it was clear I had an entourage.

"You should all come up to the house and have some lunch. We can talk more there. Better than being out in the open."

I wasn't going to disagree, but I was surprised by the frostiness in her voice and the hard look that appeared on her face. She didn't look at me again but turned to walk back the way she'd come.

I didn't move, staring at her back as she retreated from me.

"Go after her. She bears scars from shadow catchers," Neritas whispered, now at my side. He calmly pointed to the marks on the backs of her shoulders.

I exhaled, realizing what the marks on the front of her arms and around her hands must have been. My mother had fought the demons many times and not always came away unscathed. No wonder she didn't want danger being brought to her.

With a nod of gratitude to my friend, I strode off after her, raising my head and hoping I had what it took to take over whatever role was needed of our kind. If I could handle it, I was going to make sure she was done fighting, and if I could manage it, I would make sure that she didn't feel alone. I was an adult now, and it was time I took up the responsibility she had placed down.

Neritas dissuaded anyone else from walking, and all three cars slowly drove past us to the farmhouse I saw in the distance as I hurried to catch up to my mother.

She slowed when she realized I was still behind and everyone else had gone off ahead, but she didn't stop and only glanced back at me a couple of times until I caught up.

"I'm sorry. This probably isn't what you were expecting. I admit, I thought you would be angrier." She kept looking ahead, a sad look still behind her eyes.

"I might have been if I were younger and didn't know what I do now," I replied.

"You've been in the city near LA, Reijo tells me."

"Yes. Though I'm not sure what to make of it after living so long among humans."

"You don't like it?"

"I don't like that they hide away and pretend there is no problem."

My mother sighed when I said this and looked even sadder. Her head drooped and she closed her eyes briefly. Almost as suddenly as the emotion had come, it went again, and she looked back up and ahead.

"What?" I asked. "You think I've made a wrong judgment?"

"No. You've made the right one. The one we hoped you'd come to on your own."

"We?" I asked. So many questions were forming in my head that I barely knew where to begin with any of them. How did I explain everything to her and get all the information I wanted? Each thing she told me gave me three more questions.

"Your father and I. He wanted you to understand how important it was to protect human life too. How much they also matter." She finally looked at me, a wry smile on her face.

"But this makes you sad now?"

"A little. You are so young, and there's such a huge burden on your shoulders. When we had you, we hoped that you'd never have to carry it alone. We..." She shook her head, and her voice trailed off as she continued walking.

I didn't speak, not sure what to say. I had no idea what

had happened, but it seemed there were reasons I hadn't even dreamed of for why they had given me the life they had. And it appeared that my mother regretted some of it. That she had expected me to be angry about it. All I could wonder was what it must have been like for her.

A part of me had always assumed that if my parents were alive, they would have been happy and wouldn't have cared what had happened to me. I'd assumed they would have been doing their own thing and living their own lives and would have no regrets. Because if they did regret it, they would have come for me.

To find such clear regret but know she hadn't come to rescue me—that was a scenario I hadn't considered.

I'd imagined arguments and cold logic behind colder decisions, but not pain and fear. Not resignation, and definitely not an older, frail woman who looked like someone I might become if I continued down the route I was on if I couldn't find a way to a better future for all the races on earth.

"Your father would be proud of you. If he'd seen you and the way you wear those, he'd have smiled at me and told me it was all worth it."

"You don't agree?" I asked, wondering if she'd admit what she'd been hinting at.

"I did once. A part of me still does. But it doesn't matter. I made him a promise, and it is done. Only time will show if it was worth it."

The wisdom in her words, coupled with the pain in her voice, hit my heart so hard that I almost stopped breathing. A single tear tracked down her cheek, but her head stayed high, and she kept walking forward.

In that moment, I forgave them. Both of them, but especially her.

In that moment, I knew she had done her best to do what was right. She had done what she thought would give me the best chance of survival but also make me the best I could be.

She had sacrificed what she wanted to give me a chance.

"I'll make it worth it," I replied, not knowing what else I could give her but wanting to ease her pain.

Finally, she stopped, turning to me so suddenly I stuttered to a halt.

She took my hand in much the same way Ben did and looked deep into my eyes.

"You have a long path ahead of you, and I'm sorry, but there will be pain. And at times, it will feel as if it's more than you can bear. You'll feel as if you are going to break and the world around you is going to shatter along with you. You'll be so tired of fighting, of doing what's right, that you'll yearn to be able to put down your arms and stop for just a minute. But you won't. You won't break, and you won't give up. You'll carry on, and you'll do your part. And the world will see another day, and another, most of the people in it having no clue what you've done for them."

"That doesn't sound like just my journey," I replied, knowing I'd already felt some of that, and faced it in the past and expected to face it again.

"It's your legacy. The path of all those before you and all those who will follow you."

I had no response to that. None at all. I knew what I'd promised, and I was getting some idea of what was being asked of me. Despite it all, a small part of me wanted to run from this madness now while everyone else was in a car somewhere outside a farmhouse and only one person was close enough to stop me.

My mother stood in front of me, waiting as if she understood and she was giving me the chance to do so. Letting me decide for myself here and now, while no one else could influence me. I knew then that it was my choice. If I went one way, I could embrace my future as a dragon leader and in the fight against the darkness of the world.

Or I could go the other way and disappear. I had a feeling the money wouldn't stop coming, but it wouldn't matter either way. I could go get a job somewhere and start again. Forget I was ever a dragon and live a normal life.

After a few more seconds, I turned and took the first step toward the farmhouse. Not because the world needed me, not because my friends were that way or because my mother would tell me more if I did.

I walked toward my future because I wanted to know what I was made of. I wanted to know who I could become.

CHAPTER SEVENTEEN

With my mother beside me, it felt as if the world was somehow brighter than before. I wasn't alone in the same way. I'd had Ben and my friends, but this was something different. She was the same color as me, and she was strong.

Mostly she was just there. Beside me. Something I'd have hoped for but would never have dared ask for in the past. I had a mother who loved me.

"You must have some good friends," she said as we got a little closer to the farmhouse and we saw them all getting out of the cars. Reijo was leading them inside, but several refused to go.

I grinned at Neritas, Flick, Ben, and Capricia waiting outside. It was just like them to make sure that I was safe while still trying to give me the space I needed. Almost immediately, it confirmed that I had made the right decision. If nothing else, I wasn't doing any of those things alone.

"Tell me of your life. Do you like it?" Mom walked slower, her eyes brightening a little.

Appreciating the interest, I told her of how I had been adjusting to life in the city and how Neritas and Flick had been acting like my guards while Ben had become my legal guardian in her absence. A part of me hoped she would immediately volunteer to be there for me and come back to the city with me, but she didn't.

I wasn't finished with telling her everything I felt I ought to when I reached the house and everyone else.

Introducing everyone became my next task, but I noticed that my mother was now more friendly and eager to talk to them all, especially Neritas, Flick, and Ben. We quickly went inside and found Reijo already setting out lunch in a dining room off the large kitchen near the back of the farmhouse.

The house was old-fashioned but tidy and well-kept. Here and there, I noticed items that weren't as human as they ought to have been, some of them clearly magical. A human would consider it an average country house.

We all helped set the table and a spread of various foods for lunch. It was almost as if Reijo had expected lots of visitors, and I wondered if they had prepared it for us or if they had bought it hoping for something like this. It seemed strange when Reijo had sat in the diner at breakfast and let us go to the effort of getting lots more food.

I wondered what they thought might happen after this. I wanted my mother to come back with me. Just having another red dragon around would be a huge gain in my life, and I didn't want to lose her so soon after gaining her. It was clear that we had a lot to talk about.

While we ate, my mother sat on one side of me, and Flick and Neritas flanked us. Neritas sat on my mother's side.

"You remind me of a dragon I used to know," she said to him. "Used to dress a bit like you. Had a similar confidence. You're a green dragon, right?"

"Yes, green. My father was Kreanta."

"And your mother?"

"Viridian."

I paused, grateful that I wasn't the only dragon whose name had a distinct correlation to my color.

"Ah, yes, Viridian. You are similar to her. I remember her well. There was a quiet confidence in her that I liked. I'm sorry for your loss."

"Thank you. I didn't get to know her well, but I've only heard good things about her."

"From what Scarlet tells me, she would be proud of you. She had that similar rebellious streak. Loved people, had a rocky start in life, but she made everything she did count."

Everyone listened as Sienna's gentle voice spoke of something that meant a lot to Neritas too.

"Sounds a lot like your daughter as well," he shot back. His mouth twitched up into a smile with it, but it didn't reach his eyes. They had sadness in them, and I knew he was deflecting, trying to get the focus off himself.

"That I can well believe. A hotheaded red dragon who has grown up in a tough environment surrounded by humans and still being little more than a rebellious teenager in some ways." It was my mother's turn to smile as she looked at me.

I wasn't sure what to make of such an assessment. It

wasn't wrong, but it also wasn't necessarily very flattering. I could only see amusement in her eyes, though, as if that was exactly who I was meant to be and it made me perfect. The feeling it stirred in me was strange. Was I being accepted as I was? Was this what that felt like?

With nothing to compare it to, I had to let the feeling sit with me and continue to eat.

Neritas started talking about what life was like in the city for the three of us, and Flick, Ben, and I soon joined in. We all talked loads about the flying lessons.

"Jared is still teaching?" Mother asked, her eyebrows going up.

I nodded.

"Good. He's a good dragon. Knows what he's doing. I bet that means you can really fly, the three of you, if he's letting you have extra lessons and making an extra effort. He was always that kind of soul. Helps everyone reach their potential and gives everyone a chance."

I heard the wistfulness in her voice, and once again, I felt the hope flutter in my heart that she might come back to the city with me, but I didn't dare bring it up yet.

Instead, Flick told her of how some of my earlier lessons had been tough. How I'd had to learn to outfly most of the city's dragons to get away from the bullies. Although I didn't appreciate being outed as being picked on or for having loads of issues, I heard the excitement and joy as Flick bragged about me being able to fly as well as he could.

"Thank you, you two." Mother turned to Neritas and Flick in turn. "You've both shown that you care a lot about Scarlet and are willing to face danger at her side. It will help me sleep easier each night from now on to know she has such good dragons with her. It will make her path easier than I feared it might be."

The seriousness of her words took everyone by surprise, but I was grateful that she approved of my friends. So many parts of me were vying for attention and for my mother to take interest. I had thought the other orphans were silly for voicing such things and that it was a waste of time to be so sentimental, but I felt it all too, now that I was confronted with the knowledge of a mother.

As soon as everyone had finished eating, Reijo rose and started to pack the remainder of the food away. Mother got up to take dishes to the kitchen as well, but Neritas took them off her.

"Let us do this. You must have lots to talk with Scarlet about. The two of you should get as much time together as possible. We'll tidy." Neritas walked away with the dishes before she could respond in any way.

The moment she recovered, she looked at me and nodded. "I have wanted to say so many things over the years. Come, let me show you some of the things I have kept."

She reached out slowly and took my hand to give it a squeeze. I gripped it back, liking the way it felt different from Ben's and knowing it had been extended with the same sense of warmth. It was a gesture that made me feel as if the world was going to be okay. As if we would get through what we needed to and come out the other side.

Although she soon let go again, part of us remained connected, and I eagerly followed as she led up the sturdy wooden staircase to the next floor. She walked down a small corridor, past several open and shut doors, a couple of bedrooms, and a bathroom before she stopped at one of the closed doors.

After glancing at me again, she opened it and walked inside.

"This is where I have lived, cried, laughed, dreamed, and hoped almost every night since I last saw you," she said, her eyes growing moist for a few seconds while she looked around it.

I felt a mix of emotions as I followed her inside. Although I had no memories of her, I knew I hadn't been a baby when she'd given me up. The orphanage had told me that I'd been given up as a young girl. I had no memories before that day.

"I know you must have many questions for me, and I have more than a few for you, but I get the impression from Reijo and what you've said so far today that you wish to prove your heritage. To make it clear that you are the rightful dragon queen," Mother said as she sat on the edge of the bed, a cornflower-blue comforter spread out over it neatly.

I sank down beside her, my shock at her words making me mute again. She waited and took my hand again, cupping it in hers.

"Am I the queen? Aren't you?"

She shook her head. "I'm not completely pure. In some ways, it was your father's downfall. He loved me, and others thought he shouldn't. I have a small amount of blue in my family line, and it makes it difficult. You came out as red as your father, however. He knew you would be. Knew the little off-color in me wouldn't change the power flowing in his line."

"Let me guess. That fractured some already tense relationships." I didn't hide my disdain for the pettiness of it all. My mother nodded. "So, my father was king, and you can't be a queen?"

"Exactly. But you are the next in line, and I have what the dragon elders will need to accept it."

"If they didn't accept you as a suitable wife, what makes you think they will accept me as a suitable heir?" I asked, wondering if some of the animosity toward red dragons stemmed from this information.

"There is no guarantee, but if you're going to save the world, you're going to have to make them accept you for who you are. You have to find a way to unite them behind a red dragon once more."

I exhaled, not sure I liked the idea still. Did other heroes in legends gone by and those born to rule or with family responsibilities ever wish they didn't have to walk into those destinies?

My mother took my silence as acceptance and got up to go to the dresser nearby. She pulled out a small journal and, from among its pages, a birth certificate of some kind. It wasn't like the usual ones issued in the US. I had my version of that already. This one was written in the dragon language, something I was getting better at reading.

I took it, seeing her name and mine on it. But the name that mattered to everyone in the dragon world was the name in the father's box and the title attached to it. The king. I was the king's daughter.

"Neritas will be happy," I said, not sure what else to utter. This wasn't something I'd thought I wanted, but I knew part of me did. Part of me knew I could make a difference. Someone needed to. That someone might as well be me.

"It's a double-edged sword. It has its benefits too. There will be times when you will love being royalty, trust me."

I saw the mischievous grin on her face and wondered what had caused it, but I didn't get a chance to ask before she was up on her feet again. This time she went to a small cupboard and pulled out a box. It was covered in dust and taped up with tape so old that it came off with no trouble, falling apart with ease.

After coughing a little and sneezing on all the kicked-up dust, we gently opened it up together, and the box sat between us.

"This is everything I have of your father's. It's only right that it comes to you now."

Immediately I made a mental note to see what was most sentimental to my mother and get her to keep it. If he loved her enough to risk his throne over being with her, and she had loved him enough to keep a promise to him for decades after his death, even though it hurt her, I couldn't take all the keepsakes.

Inside the box was one thing that I hadn't expected. A crown. It was more delicate than I'd have thought, but it was a strange design, and it took me a moment to realize that a human head wasn't meant to wear it. This was a crown for a dragon to wear.

"I'm sorry, something that valuable should be kept in a safe, not a box, but no one knew that I had it..." She shrugged.

None of it bothered me, but I noticed that it wasn't the only thing in there. I gently reached for it and lifted it up and out of the way to get to the rest of the items. A strange brooch that shifted oddly in the light, almost as if it didn't want to be looked at, caught my eye. It was black, in the shape of a dragon, with several gemstones embedded in it.

"Now, this you should definitely have. It will aid you in combat." She pulled it out for me and immediately pinned it to my sweatshirt near my left shoulder. "It suits you even better than your father. He always used to try and give it to me, but he always needed it more, and I wanted him to be safe."

I didn't need to ask her what it did. It seemed to reach out to me and connect with my mind all on its own. It felt familiar, a lot like the sword and shield I'd found, but this was solely about my magic. It drew on it all on its own, and I was pretty sure it did something to the area around me.

"Go look in the mirror," my mother said. "It will help."

I got up and hurried over to the floor-length mirror in the corner of the room. I gasped when I saw that I didn't appear to completely be there.

"If you concentrate, you can get it to make you sort of invisible. You can still be seen by anyone really looking for you, especially in broad daylight, but standing still in front of a mirror will allow the device time to adjust, and you'll have no reflection. And it only gets better in the dark. You can move about entirely invisibly."

It was a gift I couldn't believe existed and a magical item that must have been invaluable.

Almost immediately, I reached to take it off and hand it back to her.

"No, you need it more than I do. Your father made the mistake of insisting I keep that the day he died. I won't let the same thing happen twice. If I die, the world can still be saved. If you die, however..."

I gulped, not liking that thought. I didn't want to be that selfish or cavalier with my friends.

"I know that's not an easy thing to live with. When I carried you, your father told me that I was just as important, and I know it took all my control sometimes to let someone else put themselves in danger to keep me safe. But you need to remember your future and that I choose to keep you alive to do my part in saving the world. Only one red dragon can unite the dragon community and keep the gate sealed, but any dragon can help, any dragon can protect, and any dragon can lend their magic, time, and skills. Let them play their part. Let them do what they're good at. Or you rob them of their destiny as well."

"It seems like there's a fine line between that and being cavalier with others' lives."

"There is," my mother replied and held out her arms. "But you know how I got all these, don't you?"

"By not being cavalier with others' lives."

"Exactly. You are still one of the only dragons who can face the demons in direct combat."

"But you can as well?"

"Yes. I can draw on the magic of others and combine it as you can. Your father showed me how. It's a magic known only to the royal line and their honor guards."

"I've met one of those. The chief one, in fact."

"You've met Alitas?" Her eyes widened.

"Yes. He helped me fight shadow catchers when I was taken to see the gate for myself."

"It sounds as if there is still a lot for you to tell me of your adventures so far, my child."

I nodded and moved back to the bed as I tried to put my appearance back to normal and switch off the device. It resisted a little, but only because it seemed to be brimming full of magic and impatient to be used.

"I would love to hear of your adventures sometime as well."

"There will be plenty of time for that too. Now I have found you, we will spend plenty of time together, I hope."

I had no objection to such an idea. It was everything I wanted right now.

Trying to think of where we might begin, I noticed my mother suddenly look toward the window, her forehead creasing.

I didn't need to ask her what it was. Only a few seconds later, I felt it at the edge of my mind too. The presence of something evil.

"Danger." She got up and put the crown back in the box along with my dragon birth certificate. She thrust it into my arms and ushered me from the room.

CHAPTER EIGHTEEN

It had only taken five minutes for all of us to get back into the three vehicles, my mother thankfully keeping calm and suggesting we head to a restaurant she knew where we could get food and feel safer surrounded by humans. Although shadow catchers had attacked when a human was around now and then, they didn't appear to want to.

On top of that, I was sure that Fintar had only ever appeared as a human and operated when humans hadn't been around. It was knowledge that my mother backed up. They would attack if humans were around, but only if there was some confidence that the humans wouldn't believe it or would be questioned, like the one coming into the bar. Or if they thought they might succeed in killing the humans too.

So, we were hoping for at least some protection by mingling with humans. Although I understood the logic and could agree that Fintar, at least, had been careful around humans, there was still a lack of care about hurting innocent bystanders. And humans could come and go. I couldn't think of anywhere we could go where we would be surrounded by humans all the time.

Not sure what else to do at this point, and still blown away by the box I carried under the arm not holding my shield, I let myself be ushered back into a car.

I wanted to ride with my mother, but Reijo's car had less room now that we'd added some of her stuff, and she insisted that she could keep herself safe if she knew I was surrounded by dragons who would protect me. It wasn't until she also pointed out that we could protect more of our friends in separate cars that I accepted her reasoning.

As the car carrying my mother pulled away, the anxious thought of her speeding off in a way that meant I couldn't follow plagued my mind, but Reijo drove sensibly, and we soon formed a three-car convoy again, heading west for the first time in ages.

By the time we'd been driving half an hour and had taken several turns in different directions, I was pretty sure that we had doubled back on ourselves several times and made it hard for anyone to follow us. As far as I could tell, we had also put the demons far behind us again.

Once more, I wondered how they had found us when we had been so careful. What was giving our location away?

I considered all my companions, trying to work out if any of them might be helping Fintar. I couldn't be sure it was any of them, and the thought of any one of them betraying me didn't make any sense. There had to be another explanation, and I made it my first thought to mention when I was with my mother again. Hopefully when we were alone. I was clearly missing something, and she might be able to help.

The restaurant turned out to be in the middle of a shopping mall. It was busy with afternoon shoppers, but the restaurant was quiet.

With it being too early to eat after lunch, we only bought snacks and drinks and made ourselves comfortable. While many of my companions were helping with drinks or using restrooms or various other tasks, and Jace stepped away to make a phone call to the dragons in her world, I took the opportunity to ask my mother what she thought.

For a few seconds, she looked thoughtful.

"That is a tough thing to suspect. I can see why you might wonder if they do indeed show up everywhere you go that is not in the city, but these people are loyal to you. If it is one of them, then it is someone very clever and very good at hiding their true feelings."

"You said that my father choosing you caused controversy and that it divided people. Could that be playing a part in this?"

"Possibly, but it would be incredibly low for a dragon to take the side of the demons. A human maybe, but not a dragon." I frowned, not sure I understood what my mother was saying.

"Fintar, the handler who tricked me, was part dragon and part...something else. Ben implied he had once been a dragon."

"Are you sure?"

I nodded. People were rejoining us, and my window to talk to my mother about the group had vanished. For now, I still had no idea how the shadow catchers could be finding us, but I needed to find out, or I was likely to be on the run until Fintar, or whoever was after me, got lucky.

We ate together, everyone on edge, no one quite relaxing.

"What is the plan now?" Capricia asked. "I don't want to be out here and in danger any longer than necessary."

Although I didn't disagree with her, I also didn't want to rush anything, and I knew my mother might have more to say to me. We hadn't had much time earlier. If I was returning to the city to claim a throne, I wanted to make sure I did it the right way, with as much understanding as possible about my current circumstances and the historic events leading to my father's death.

"There are places we can go that are safer. A dragon refuge nearby. It has magical systems that will keep us from being detected easily and would give us warning if more demons were nearby."

"That sounds like a great place to go," Jace blurted out her words with an irritation I hadn't expected. "Why aren't we there already?"

"Because I don't know if I can trust all of you yet," my mother replied with a snap, making it clear she was not used to anyone taking that tone with her.

I stifled a grin at the temper I recognized as the one I sometimes displayed and glanced at Jace surreptitiously. The young woman raised an eyebrow and paused but seemed to be okay enough with what had happened.

"How can we help you trust us?" Ben asked before anyone could speak.

It was another indicator that he was far more of a diplomat than I was, and I was grateful for it. It was hard to know what to say when there were so many angles and agendas at the table.

My mother frowned and looked around at everyone at the table.

"I want to know about all of you. What part do you play in Scarlet's life? Why, out of everyone that could be here, are you the dragons who came along for the journey? What have you done to aid my daughter and help her stay alive? With the exception of Merrik, who has guarded red dragons in my past long before all this, I know little of any of you."

"Well, I can make that simple in my case. And Tim's." Harriet held her hand up. "I had never met Scarlet until two days ago. But Jace said she needed our help and needed dragons who were eager to give shadow catchers hell rather than running from them for a change. And she trusts us not to say anything."

"Thank you for your honesty." My mother gave Harriet and Tim a nod, her eyes flicking to the obvious bandage on Harriet's shoulder.

"For people who have only known me for a day or two, they've also already fought beside me," I added. "And done so bravely. Both of them."

Of course, there was a chance one of these people was betraying me. But I felt it wasn't them. Or at least, it wasn't just them. If I was being betrayed, it was someone who had been closer to me. Someone who had a better idea of where I was at all times. A part of me hoped that my mother could pick up on who it might be if I gave her enough information. And I might be able to figure it out if I talked about it with her too.

In an instant, I decided to give it a go and reveal everything. It was going to give everyone there all the information as well, but if one of them was betraying me, by this point they knew a fair bit or could put it all together anyway. I couldn't hide what most of this meant.

Over the course of the next hour, while we continued to drink and eat more food, I told everyone my story. I left a couple of things out—I still didn't mention the journals that Anthony had left, but I talked about the trail he'd left us and how he knew something we hadn't discovered yet. No one but Ben knew as much as I said, and even Neritas and Flick, to whom I had given a similar rundown a few weeks earlier, didn't have all this detail.

They hadn't known that Capricia and others had rescued me and Ben when we'd found Anthony, or that I'd wounded a shadow catcher then. None of them knew that I had fled from them before knowing I was a dragon.

There were lots of pieces of information that some of them knew, but others didn't. Everyone learned something, my mother most of all.

She listened through the whole tale, not saying a word but nodding in the right places. Now and then, one of my friends added something I either hadn't been aware of or I'd missed.

Recounting everything made me realize how far I had already come. How many times I had faced the shadow catchers and survived, and how many people had helped me along the way. Not all of them were here either.

It was only as I was coming to the end of my story and talking about Neritas finding my sword and shield and beginning to train that Ben chimed in.

"You didn't tell me that Capricia had been helping or that you were fighting shadow catchers sometimes during those moments."

For a few seconds, I stopped talking, surprised that I hadn't told Ben and equally puzzled about him not having figured it all out by himself. I was sure that I'd have told him enough to make it clear what my evenings had been spent on. But there had been so much going on the last few days, and we had been talking so much about trying to meet Reijo that I must not have mentioned it.

"Nor so many nights." He frowned, and his reaction confused me.

"What else would I have been doing with Neritas and Flick in the evenings?" I asked.

"The normal sorts of things young women do with men in the evenings," Capricia replied for Ben, and everyone laughed as my cheeks grew hotter and hotter.

I couldn't look at Neritas and Flick as I tried to compose myself. They were friends, and I got the feeling I had somehow insulted both of them because I hadn't considered the possibility everyone thought was the most obvious.

"Given the number of shadow catchers that chase you, I understand," Ben said as he reached for my hand and gave it a familiar squeeze. It helped me refocus, although I was irritated that I had been derailed by talk of boys and what I was expected to have done in their company. I was fighting for my life on a regular basis. Romance had been one of the furthest things from my mind.

In the end, however, it was only a small detail, and it came close to the end of my story. I finished talking about the events that had led us to meeting Reijo and coming to find my mother, grateful that everyone there knew about all of it.

When I finished speaking, it was still. Everyone waited, not daring to speak.

"That is quite an adventure. And one of many parts. You've all done well to come this far and support each other. I think I understand better why all of you are here before me, and we are meeting like this." My mother looked around at everyone one last time.

"It means a lot to us to be here beside Scarlet," Ben said. "All of us have a reason to have sought this as well. In one way or another. None of us want to keep running and hiding, and none of us want to sit back and do nothing but live in a refuge city while the world falls apart around us."

Mother met his gaze last and held it the longest while he spoke. It was only as she continued to stare at him that I realized what she must be wondering. Ben was the only person who had been there or known where I was at all times, with the exception of the few instances I had been on the beach with my friends.

I paused, searching through my memory of whether I had told him what I was doing with Neritas and Flick. He'd known something because of the sword and shield. Had I told him enough that he could have sent the shadow catchers after me? Was that what my mother was getting at with her lingering gaze?

Before I could say anything else, she nodded, but she also looked at him as if she trusted him now. Was all of this just a coincidence?

"Thank you all for keeping Scarlet safe," she said a few

seconds later, cutting through my thoughts. "For not giving up. And for not buying into the lies that some dragons have been peddling. There are some truths of my own I have to share, but I am tired now. Years of a difficult life and magic use beyond anything that many of you could imagine has meant that I tire easily. It is time to get some rest for the evening. We'll talk more about serious things tomorrow, in the light of day, where it belongs."

No one argued as we all trooped back to the cars and continued our journey. Reijo headed out of the area on a road north, followed by the other two vehicles. It was time to find out what kind of refuge was nearby. Wherever we were going, it was new to all of us, and the anticipation and the reflection on everything that I'd told people in my recent story made us all quiet.

It was going to be an interesting day tomorrow.

CHAPTER NINETEEN

It took about half an hour to reach our destination. A lake stood in the middle of nowhere. A small hut by the shore was the only building I could see for miles. We pulled up beside it, making me wonder if anyone owned it or looked after it.

As I got out of the car, I closed my eyes and felt as far out for danger as I could. When I opened my eyes, I realized everyone was staring at me. Then I caught them glancing at my mom as she drew their attention.

Without consulting each other or having each other as a frame of reference, we had gotten out of the cars and done exactly the same thing. And with the same result, no doubt. We were safe. At least for now.

I walked toward her slowly, not sure she had noticed our mirrored actions as she gave Reijo a nod and he went over to the building nearby. When we got closer, and the moon slipped out from behind a cloud, I realized it wasn't just a bog-standard wooden beach hut but also a boat shed of some kind set right on the water.

Reijo opened the shed with a key he pulled from his back pocket. Two large rowing boats sat side by side inside it. I estimated that it was going to be a tight squeeze to get all of us into them but that we would fit if we left some of our supplies in the vehicles.

Although I was a little nervous about doing that, I wasn't leaving anything of value behind. Food and camping equipment was the bulk of it. Everything else that mattered to me, the journals from Anthony, the sword, the shield, and now the box from my mother and the brooch on my shoulder, was coming with me.

I was not letting any of that go anywhere but with me or, in the journals' case, Ben.

We quickly loaded the boats with the essentials and got in too. I sank to the bench in one boat while my mother guarded the other and was grateful when I realized I wouldn't be required to row.

I wasn't even the person who needed to steer. I was sitting right in the center of the boat in front of Neritas, who was rowing for my boat, while Ben manned the tiller. Yet again, I was being kept safe, but I wasn't about to argue with that either.

The day had been eventful in so many ways, and although the evening wasn't late, I was exhausted. I didn't have much drive to do anything but enjoy the view and the motion of the boat through the water.

I watched my mother and her boat now and then. Cios rowed for her while Reijo steered. We'd only taken the supplies we'd need until morning. I wasn't sure what would happen after that. It was all now up to my mother and what she thought was best.

Capricia kept looking around us, still clutching the shield I had charged for her. Many of the others had put theirs down, feeling safe enough now that they had two red dragons with them who could both sense the enemy and fight them.

I had to admit I felt better knowing I could face them now and not face them alone. It was as if some of the pressure had been removed, but I also got the impression Mother would avoid fighting them and would run if she could, rather than kill them. And with all her scars, I wasn't sure I blamed her.

Our boats moved through the water as it got darker. Mother and I soon had to light the way, making ourselves glow just enough that the water could be seen and we could see each other. I didn't know how far we had to go or how Mother knew if we were still going in the right direction, but she didn't appear to falter, and her eyes remained fixed forward.

Almost out of habit, but partially from curiosity, I felt around for what I could sense with my mind, wondering if I would be able to feel other good things the way I had picked up on her. As far as I could tell, we were alone. If nothing else, it was reassuring to not have demons to worry about. And I had to admit there was a benefit to living out on a lake.

After what must have been an hour and a half or so of rowing, when Neritas was tiring and our boat had slowed a little, a shape loomed up from the dark ahead. It was an island or perhaps the other side of the lake.

Reijo steered the front boat to one side, deviating for the first time from the same straight line. Ben followed with enough skill that we weren't left too far behind and had some chance of making sure we didn't hit anything we shouldn't.

We continued for a couple more minutes as the shape got larger and more pronounced. It was strange not to be the one leading or knowing where I was going, but I had been shown so many things over the last few months. I guessed this was just another adventure.

I could only hope that this one had a better ending than the last.

As we got closer, I noticed rocks stuck up here and there, and Mother and Reijo were somehow guiding the boats in between them, following some pathway that only they knew. Now and then, Mother would reach out one of her hands on either side of her and get Reijo to steer that way.

This was where it grew trickier. Ben needed to follow, but he couldn't turn right away. He had to try to follow their exact path. I moved nearer the front of the boat and concentrated on it, making it glow on the outside and down by the water level.

It had the desired effect and lit up the rocks a little better so Ben could do his best to avoid them.

I also lowered myself and shifted to one side, with Capricia doing the same on the other side so we could push ourselves away from any rocks we got too close to.

Although our methods were a little unorthodox, they helped our less-than-practiced crew get our boat safely after my mother's.

Time seemed to slip past as we traveled farther than I could have imagined in this way. Whoever had found this island and a route through the rocks must have been a very skilled boatman. Or woman.

Making a mental note to ask my mother, I gently pushed our front away from another rock we wouldn't have made it past when Ben turned a little too much. My arms were hurting, and the magic used to cast the light we needed was adding to the tiredness I felt.

The thought popped into my head that I could suck a little magic from the dragons around me and use it to make myself feel better, but after everything we had done that day and how little we had slept, I was sure that they would be feeling as tired as I was. I couldn't do that to them.

Finally, my mother guided the boat to turn and pointed at something ahead. I heard her muttering but couldn't make out what she said. Her boat coasted as Cios stopped rowing.

Reijo steered them into what looked like a natural bank, and Tim practically sprang from the front of the boat and onto the shore.

Harriet threw him a rope, and Neritas also stopped rowing and let us slow. We grew closer to my mother's boat, but it was only gentle progress, and Tim and Cios were soon moving down the bank to help us get close.

We didn't need to get as close as the first boat. Capricia threw the rope to Tim, and he helped pull us in closer. In less than a minute, our boat was secure against the bank, and we were all fetching out the supplies we had brought with us.

"Welcome to an island that is probably one of the best-kept secrets in dragon history. I have brought you all here in the cover of night, and we will leave again before dawn. No harm will come to anyone while here, and humans cannot find us." Mother fought back a smile and stretched out her hands. In the dark, we couldn't see much, but I got the impression it was an impressive island in some way.

I blinked as my mother lowered her hands and put out all the light.

"Let yourself go dark," she said to me a fraction of a second later. "And your sword and shield as well."

Although I wasn't sure what good it would do us, I had trusted her so far. No sooner had I done so than I realized that a strange plant on the ground seemed to give off a small amount of light. It lit the edges of the cove we were in, climbing a hill on either side, but most importantly, it lit a path to some steps and up beyond it.

Feeling as if I had stepped into an enchanted fairyland, I climbed after my mother and led the way with her.

The plants and the area they lit up were beautiful, and I could hear wildlife in the background. No birds sang, but we heard the occasional twitter, flutter of wings, and sound of movement in the sky above. On top of that, crickets chirped, and something bigger rustled plants here and there.

"None of the wildlife here will hurt us," Mother said when the rest of the group hesitated past a particularly active bush.

"How did you find this place?" I asked my mother as we climbed the steps. My heart rate picked up though it wasn't all that steep, just winding and long.

"Your father showed it to me and made me learn the route in. Of course, he showed me by day. But only royal dragons and those sworn to them, and part of the honor guard, are meant to come here, and even fewer know the route in. I've broken the rules here today, but I've done so with the knowledge that I've made it very hard for anyone to follow. Even a handler would struggle to get to us if they knew exactly where we were."

An interesting set of secrets. I had a lot to learn about my family, it seemed.

I had so many more questions still, and this latest revelation had only given me more, but this wasn't the time and place for them. We all needed sleep, especially if we would be starting out early in the morning.

The steps led to a plateau that was open to the elements on three sides and bordered by more luminescent plants. It had more rock against the fourth edge and a small staircase with smaller and tighter steps that wound higher in the middle.

Mother ignored this and encouraged everyone to find a spot to lie down.

"We can make a fire and eat and sleep here," she said. "It will be perfectly safe, and we won't need to worry about anyone seeing or noticing the fire."

Again I wondered where we were and whether there was danger nearby. I moved a little farther onto the flatter area and closed my eyes. Almost immediately, I felt a presence up ahead and up, but it didn't feel bad or as if it was something to be wary or uneasy about.

Thankfully, I sensed no evil. Whatever had been trying to follow us, it couldn't come here, and it hopefully wouldn't be able to sense us either.

Before I could do anything else, my group fanned out

and got to work building a fire. Mother showed them where to find a few basic supplies, and I was left standing beside Ben.

"Are you sure you did the right thing letting everyone here know so much?" Ben asked.

"I'm not sure, but I know that I had to try and make this work, and Mother was also aware that one of them might not be as trustworthy as we needed them to be."

"Or multiple someones." Ben looked at them all. I knew he had a point, but I also knew that I had kept the most important part from them at this point. Anthony still possibly knew more, and we still hadn't figured out what.

It hadn't occurred to me that it could be more than one. I had been looking for the first person who could have truly betrayed me, but it was possible that several were working with Fintar or someone like him.

"I had to try to find out if they were trustworthy or not. I thought Mother could help." I shrugged, not sure what else to say and too tired to want to do much but go to sleep. The staircase was nagging at me as well, however. But Mother was on her way back—I saw her dim luminescence coming my way.

"This group could all be against you for all we know," Ben replied, still not happy.

"They aren't. Not in the way you mean," Mother said as she joined us. "I wouldn't have let any of you come here if there was a traitor in your midst feeding information to the shadow catchers or a handler."

This seemed to help Ben a little, but it made me grin the most. My mother seemed to be certain.

"Forgive me for questioning you when you are clearly

very experienced in these matters. But how do you know for sure?" he asked.

"I know these things in many ways. I can feel no danger. None at all. None of these dragons harbors any desire to harm the others, and you all get along for the most part. But also, I studied many of them during my daughter's story, and it is clear that many of them are supportive and have faced dangers together. On top of that, none of them could have been the person to bring Fintar to you on every occasion. None of them knew enough at the right times except for the two of you."

This was partially news to me and partly not. It was true that I had worked out that none of them alone could have betrayed me, but I hadn't considered that they could be working as a team. It might make sense for Jace and her party to have been, but as they had pointed out, Tim and Harriet were new, and I was sure they were here to kill shadow catchers and make hell. They weren't going to put themselves in more danger. They were here because danger kept showing up.

If Jace had brought them on board, it made no sense for her to betray us. She was making it easier for me to kill the shadow catchers. And she clearly wanted the information as much, if not more, than I did.

Cios and Merrik struck me as too honorable to do anything but fight, but I knew that was a gut reaction. Neritas and Flick had only been with me a handful of times and knew nothing of me or any of this until recently, so it couldn't be them. Capricia had been in the city for a lot of the attacks and not known of my actions or location either.

That did only leave Ben. But again, if Ben wanted these

fights and wanted me dead, he could have made it happen so much more easily and with far less risk to himself.

I exhaled, feeling more tension leave my body. None of the dragons with me were a threat. That meant something even harder to avoid was happening. Somehow Fintar and the shadow catchers were finding me on their own.

"As much as it seems to be true that none of the dragons here are a threat, there is still the danger that Anthony talked of in his journals," Ben pointed out quietly.

I hadn't yet told Mother of those, but she merely raised an eyebrow and motioned for us to follow her.

CHAPTER TWENTY

Without another word, she led us to the steps as Reijo came over.

As Reijo approached us, she told him, "Don't let anyone else follow us up here under any circumstances."

He nodded and stepped over the route once we'd passed, making sure that no one could even attempt it.

"This area is for royalty only," Mother explained when we had wound up a little higher, the steps narrower and heading up tighter.

"I question if I should leave the two of you to it, then." Ben stopped and looked back down. The plants up here no longer lit the route but had seemingly been planted to obscure it. I realized it was Mother lighting our way faintly, not the plant.

"You have taken the role of Scarlet's father in the dragon world, haven't you?" she asked, her voice even more gentle than normal. "You said you claimed her guardianship despite being a separate color to protect her, did you not?"

"Yes. I believed it was what Anthony would have done, and I knew I had to finish what he started. Something about Scarlet and protecting her was more important to him than anything else."

My mother nodded and turned to carry on, motioning once more for us to both follow.

"Then you have every right to be here as well. You are the father of a queen. You must embrace your responsibility for the good of the world."

It was my final confirmation that my birth father was gone, but it was also, on my mother's part, an acceptance of the family I had found along my journey. It was a statement of who I was. Emotions flooded me, so varied and so deep that it took all my strength to keep lifting each leg to climb the steps ahead of me.

Something drew me onward. Just as something had made me want to give up when I had approached the gate that held back the monster responsible for all the death and destruction in my life, this path made me want to rush onward. Some force encouraged me deeper and nearer the top despite the ache in my legs and the tiredness I had felt since before I started.

I glanced back at Ben a couple of times to notice that he was panting and didn't appear to be finding it as easy. Without thinking, I reached to his magic, connected to it, and fed some of mine to him, drawing on what was in my sword and shield to give the best boost I could.

He looked up at me and met my gaze, his eyes going wider.

As he picked up on what I'd given him, he gave me a nod, and I saw the pain and tiredness ease on his face. I had made this easier on him, and it brought comfort to my mind to know that giving the magic I could draw on had come as naturally to me as taking it did.

"You spoke of journals that Anthony left behind. These talk of danger?"

"Yes. He was protecting Scarlet as well, but we don't know what from."

"Possibly Fintar," I suggested. "This handler. He talked like he knew who I was on more than one occasion. And Anthony had met him in some capacity." I shuddered, thinking about the creepy handler and how he had talked to me and made me think he was a friend.

"It's possible. But he also kept you out of the city. He didn't think the city was safe either. Or thought something or someone could endanger you there."

"All the bullies who don't like red dragons." I exhaled and thought of how tough it had been at first. With Neritas and Flick as allies and more time passing, it hadn't been too bad lately, but I still bore scars on my back from the attack I'd sustained in the middle of a thunderstorm once.

"I think he meant something worse than a few misguided teenagers." Ben said it as if they hadn't hurt me, but he had a point. The context in the journals implied something worse. Something far more sinister.

"The king spoke of similar fears. It is possible that someone in the city isn't true to our kind." Mother said the words with an undercurrent of anger, almost as if she knew more than she was letting on, but she didn't elaborate, and I wasn't sure if I should ask. I didn't think it was easy for her to talk about my biological father.

With that said, there wasn't anything more we could

speculate or go over, however. The truth was that danger lurked, and we would have to be careful. None of us had enough information, and we could only do our best to survive and keep each other safe. For now, that was to continue with our path.

The next corner we came to was the sharpest yet, and it brought with it a blast of wind that almost knocked me off my feet. The path was no longer sheltered, and it flattened out with the last few steps taking us to the edge of a stone-built platform. A pillared section with rock flooring and sculptures lit up by more plants filled what appeared to be the top of the island.

"Here is where the power of the red dragons originated." Mother strode through an arch and toward a dais in the center of the pillars.

It lit up when she got closer, but she stopped on the edge of the circle and moved around it to stop on a smaller circular stone to one side. I stopped at the edge of the same circle, not sure what to do. As Ben came up beside me, Mother put out her hand.

"Do not get any closer, Ben. Follow the circle until you find another setting opposite me. Stand there. You will feel it when you are in the correct place."

Without responding, Ben did as he'd been instructed and moved around the edge of the circle to the right position. As soon as he stepped on the symbol on the ground, it lit up, and he wobbled for a moment.

"That's quite a feeling." He turned to face the dais.

I looked at each of them and the object in the middle. Small lines of light were appearing between them and the center, but they stopped at the base and didn't go any farther.

"Go on, Scarlet. Go to it."

I didn't move at first, worried about what might happen and resisting the strange impulse trying to draw me nearer. This felt a lot more serious than I expected. As if this was the moment I was accepting my birthright, if I intended to do it.

Didn't becoming a queen require more ceremony or something? I had no idea, but I knew I'd already promised my mother that I'd try to take on my responsibilities. That I would try to be a queen, simply so she could rest at last. She had clearly been a protector in the past. A fighter. Someone who took the risks others couldn't or wouldn't.

It was my turn to bear the responsibility for a while. I hoped that I wouldn't break under the strain.

With this thought and all the fear in the world that I wouldn't be strong enough, I stepped forward. It took five steps to get to the dais, and with each one I took, it brightened, lines appearing and spreading across it, forming a similar pattern to the weaponry I still had.

Instinct took over, and I put the shield down, noticing what looked like markers to put my hands on. I placed my hands on the dais and felt an instant connection to it. The magic within it reached into me, exploring and giving and taking at the same time.

I gasped but couldn't pull my hands back. My body was rooted to the spot and held in place.

"Don't fight it. It won't hurt you," Mother's voice came from my left.

"You've got this, Scarlet," Ben added.

The two of them being there brought me comfort, and I tried to relax and let whatever this was happen. Memories that weren't mine flashed in my head. Images of red dragons in crowns and humans wielding weapons. The gate, what it must have felt like to seal it, and then more thoughts. Fights, pain, pleasure, stress, delight, and the continuation.

More and more faces, both in dragon and human form, all of them red dragons, men and women, powerful and brave. Sometimes anger came to me, but the sort borne from defiance of an enemy or hurt of a loved one. Eventually, there was peace, punctuated by the powerful magic of one of my ancestors charging the gate.

Now and then, dragons were involved on Earth, in wars and famines. I saw the withdrawal from humanity as their numbers dwindled, magic protecting everyone. This feeling marched until one dragon and then a human face was left. Nothing needed to tell me that it was the face of my father. I could see something in the human form that, when added to my mother's, would make me. Familiar but not identical.

As if he were there, he looked right at me and nodded. An ache formed in my chest. A desire to know him, to not have him leave me right now. Beyond my control, the image faded, the magic receded, and the dais let my body go. I stepped back, panting as the lights gently faded and the glow returned to a gentle light.

Although I got the impression that I could have stepped forward and activated it again and perhaps sought more information or knowledge of an event in the past, I was far more aware of how tired I was now than I had been when it took control and showed me. At the same time, I felt as if I was more than I had been. It had given me something. More magic or more instinctive understanding. I wasn't sure exactly what. But I had become something I hadn't been only a few seconds before.

I turned and walked back out of the circle as both my parental figures came around the edge. They each took a hand, no one saying a word. They looked tired, but they had a light in their eyes as they looked at me and smiles on their faces. They were proud. Of that much, I was sure, but I saw something more too.

Hope.

"Come, let us return to the others and get some rest. You are queen now. Whether other dragons will recognize it or not, it is done. You bear the fate of the earth, and you are its guardian. I cannot offer you comfort, riches, or respect. But you do have the power of the dragons who took the role before you, and you will always be able to come here again and seek anything you need." Mother gave my hand a squeeze as she spoke.

I hadn't wanted this, but it seemed that I was going to have to deal with it anyway. As for riches and comfort, those were never things I sought. I'd never wanted my life to be dull or ordinary. Never wanted to live a life like others. Respect would have been helpful, though. But that was something I had a chance to earn.

Without a word, the three of us went back down the steps. This time I led the way, the route seeming to be in my memory as if I had walked down here a hundred times before. I was pretty sure that, in some way, I now had, but I had no words to describe what had just happened or what I had received in the transfer from the dais.

It took longer to go back down, with my legs complaining and the tiredness of all of us coming into play. Once again, I drew on the magic in the sword and shield I carried and fed all three of us. This time when I connected to the sword and shield, it felt as if they were old friends, familiar, and my understanding of them was different. Something about them made it easier to use and more efficient.

If nothing else, after tonight, I was going to be stronger and more capable of fighting the evil in this world. No one needed to point that out to me. But I had no idea exactly how much.

By the time we got back to the bottom, Neritas and Tim were cooking something for us all to eat over a small campfire. The smell was heavenly, though they insisted the fare was simple. I was so hungry that I didn't care.

I felt a lot of eyes on me, but no one asked what had happened or where we had gone. Everyone focused on getting close to the fire, resting, and eating. Reijo had pulled several large blankets from his car trunk and loaded them into the boats, and we draped them around our backs in groups, huddling together to help keep warm. Someone pulled out a bottle of whiskey and passed it around. It helped relax the atmosphere and calm everyone.

My mother had told me that I wouldn't come down the mountain to riches or greatness, but as I sat eating a hot stew, sandwiched between Flick and Neritas, with Ben and my mother nearby, friends talking and laughing as they swapped stories of foods and recipes that had gone both well and badly, I knew that what I had was better.

This was the sort of moment that made acquaintances into friends and friends into lifelong companions. This was what made memories to last a lifetime and forged who we were and what we stood for.

I continued to eat as I listened, grateful that I didn't need to do any more magic right now. The fire cast enough light, and everyone was calm and resting, all of us recovering already.

Now and then, I focused on the area around us, making sure I couldn't feel any evil. I was more aware of my mother than before, and I noticed I was also aware of Ben now, another glowing beacon in my mind, and I thought I might also be able to feel Neritas and Flick, but with them both sitting so close to me, I couldn't be sure that was what I was picking up on.

My mind also found it easier to reach out and try to sense evil. As if my range was longer and more precise. But there was nothing but the island and water as far as I could detect. We were safe. Safe and alone.

CHAPTER TWENTY-ONE

Someone shook me awake long before I wanted to be. I had no idea how much sleep I'd gotten, but I stretched and almost bumped into Neritas and Flick. With no tents or shelters, all of us had ended up sleeping in a huddle near the fire, with the rock wall behind us and enough blankets to keep us warm.

Still in the dark, we all got back up and finished packing everything. Reijo was already putting out the fire, taking our biggest source of light with it.

I lit up several rocks around the area, holding them bright enough that we could see to move and finish gathering our belongings, but not so bright that they illuminated anything beyond the plateau we had slept upon.

Mother appeared eager to leave. She had a frown fixed on her face as she moved here and there, helping to pick up everything we had brought with us. Only when we were heading back down the steps, laden with what was left of our supplies, did she appear to relax.

More than once, she mentioned that the average

dragon shouldn't be able to find and get to this place, but I wasn't sure how important that was. Once again, my knowledge of the dragon world appeared to be lacking, and I didn't dare ask when I had so many around me.

The dais didn't seem to have given me any greater understanding of things like this. I knew only that it was important, but not why or what the consequences would be. It was as if the dais had given me only the emotion and not the reasoning behind the knowledge. Leaving now felt right, and it felt right to be respecting the secrecy of it, but I wasn't sure from whom or why.

Everyone else was cooperative, and although many of them took a little while to truly seem awake, by the time we were back on the shore near the boats, they were all animated and talkative again.

"We're driving past a coffee shop as soon as we're back to civilization," Jace muttered while Ben and Reijo got into the boats while Neritas and Cios held them still.

I grinned, thinking of one of the perks of the human world. Coffee shops everywhere. Dragons had the beverage in the city, but it didn't appear to hold the same appeal, and it wasn't part of the same culture. It was an element of the human world I preferred.

Some mornings could only be rescued with coffee, and Jace wasn't wrong. This felt like one of them. No one should be up this early, especially not because of being hunted. It was the worst combination.

As I thought back through what I'd seen and all the emotions I'd felt in the last twenty-four hours, I was also more than ready for something that made it all a little better. Some muffins or chocolate needed to feature in my not-too-distant future too.

I didn't voice this, but got into a boat and let everyone else get in around me.

Once more, we navigated our way back out and away from the island, going through the rocks a different way from how we had arrived. The island soon receded behind us as I helped us navigate past rocks and out through a tricky patch where a moving current rushed us away.

Finally, we were out on the open lake again, a silhouette of the island behind us but otherwise lost in the night. My mother led the way again, but she needn't have bothered. It was as if I knew it now and could have directed us back here again.

I even knew when to look back to see a magic veil that hid the island kick in and watch the island disappear from view entirely. Everyone else was facing forward, so no one else noticed it, but I saw it go from there to gone and felt the difference immediately. A part of me was connected to it. Faintly and in a way that I only noticed if I looked for it.

I instinctively knew this feeling would guide me to and from it for the rest of my life and help me to see magic that hadn't been noticeable on the way in. It was as if it confused the mind, making it forget it existed.

When we were about halfway back to the shoreline, the sky began to lighten and the view around us grew. Within ten minutes, we could see what we were aiming for on the horizon. The strip of land that made up our destination. Behind us, I saw nothing but water. The lake was too big for the far edge to be seen.

I wanted to return during the day sometime in the

future, but today wasn't that day. I had all the proof I was going to get that I was the heir to the royal bloodline. I could only return to the city and tell them what I knew and unite them to power the gate.

I had a feeling that I had a lot to learn still, but some new magic would come to me instinctively. Things my ancestors could do and make happen. It was as if that basic natural use now ran through me.

When we got to shore and reloaded the cars, everyone came together between them.

"What now?" Jace asked, serious and clearly not thinking about coffee yet.

"I'd like you all to come with me back to the city," I said before anyone could reply. It was the only thing that made sense from here. "I need to convince the elders that I am who I say I am, and I think I need you all for that. I know I'd like you all by my side."

Most of them nodded, grinning or at least content, Tim and Harriet included, but Reijo looked at my mother, and Jace frowned.

"We'll come with you," my mother said and smiled, the rare gesture brightening her face in the light of dawn.

That left Jace, and I turned to her, knowing she held a lot of weight with the group thought of as terrorists in the city. Given that Capricia had recognized her, I knew I was asking a lot of her, more than I perhaps ought to, but I wanted her there and hoped to clear her name and others' when I arrived.

"I'm not accustomed to taking orders from anyone," she replied. "You only have to ask Capricia that."

"She's not wrong about that one," the city guard replied with a barking laugh.

"It's not an order. I'd like you there. You've been with me for a lot of this, and I think I can help you. Plus, there's more to learn, and you've earned knowing all that too." I met her gaze as the side of her mouth curled up, and she nodded.

"You had me at 'it's not an order,' Red, but the rest works too. Promise we can get breakfast from somewhere before we head back, though. I'm starving."

"We've got some food in the cars," Capricia pointed out.

"We'll need it if the shadow catchers reappear later in the journey," Ben replied.

"If we go somewhere where there are plenty of humans, and we don't stay long, it should be safe." Reijo pulled out his car keys and nodded to my mother to go with him.

With that settled, we headed back to the cars and split into the usual three groups. It felt strange to have a party of eleven when I was used to two. I'd started this journey not sure I wanted any company besides Ben, and now here I was, asking nine other people to stick by me. I wouldn't have objected to adding Alitas or some of the other dragons I'd met along the way, either.

I sighed as I sat between Neritas and Flick and tried to imagine what it would be like returning this time, and how I wanted to deal with whatever followed. A part of me wanted to keep hiding it. To go before the elders and simply state what I thought was the truth. To get their advice and work out what they knew.

But another part of me was sick of hiding. Sick of how

everyone in the city acted as if I was the most annoying dragon ever and I should go away and stop making their lives worse. But we had a responsibility—all of us, as a race.

On top of all that, I knew that it was my job to unite them and make them realize that the world was in danger. That part wasn't going to be easy. Hiding in the shadows, sneaking around, and trying to have secretive meetings didn't seem as if it was going to help convince them. But neither did threatening everyone or acting like a hotheaded red dragon who just wanted power. Somehow, I had to find a middle road.

Before long, we were at a large restaurant on the way back to the city. The place was part of a large row of shops and cafés with humans around. Everyone ordered quickly, and we were soon eating, talking, and trying to figure out the best strategy between us.

"I think you should just stroll in there, tell everyone that you're queen, and they can like it or lump it. You've got your mom, the crown, and we can all testify that you know how to kill demons." Jace grinned as she spoke. I didn't deny that I liked the idea, but I wasn't sure that was wise.

"The other dragons deserve to know, but they're not trusting of red dragons right now," Neritas replied, tilting his head to the side.

"But they'll have to realize that it's likely, right? That's half the reason they've all been so bratty to her. They know she's possibly royalty, and they like sticking it to her." Flick took a large bite of pancakes oozing with butter and syrup.

As they argued back and forth and different people suggested different things, I noticed that Ben and my mother were quiet. I sighed. However I did it, I wanted them to be okay with it. As much as my friends wanted to be involved, suggest what they thought was best, and help me figure it out, it was me who would be judged for it.

"Being a leader is never easy, and everyone will have an opinion on everything," my mother said quietly as she reached under the table and gave my hand a quick squeeze.

"Do what you think is best. We'll stand beside you either way. And the rest of them will as well," Ben added, almost whispering.

I nodded, not sure I could speak but grateful for the vote of confidence. Giving my emotions time to recover again, I focused on my food. I didn't want to waste the opportunity to eat well when I had no idea what my life was going to look like when I got back.

My mind imagined being arrested by the other dragons, having the whole city turn aggressive toward me, and all sorts of other nasty scenarios. It could go so many ways.

Knowing what I did of the gate and what lay behind it, however, I couldn't stay silent. I was going to have to take a risk and hope that it worked. It was time I stopped hiding that I was a queen.

With this thought, I took the last bite and finally looked up. Most of the conversation had died down or turned to other things, everyone else quickly finishing and picking up on the new mood. It wasn't up for discussion anymore.

I was about to request the bill when I felt a chill up my spine and realized that I felt a new sense of dread. It grew quickly, and I had to stand, barely able to breathe at how overwhelming it was.

Trying to concentrate, I felt Ben stand beside me and

put an arm around my waist, supporting me as I wobbled on my feet.

"What is it, Red?" Neritas asked, also getting to his feet.

I tried to focus, blinking away the strange blur in my vision. Other people were staring at me and the rest of my group, aware that something wasn't okay.

A moment later, my mother stifled a gasp and put her hand to her heart. I reached for her other hand, knowing she was feeling what I was feeling.

"They're attacking in full force," she said.

"Shadow catchers?" Jace asked as she and Capricia also got to their feet.

"Yes. Get the shields and anything else we can use," I replied, looking around at everyone and feeling how many monsters were already coming.

I didn't know how I was only now feeling it, but there were a lot of them, they were in a large circle, and they were coming closer as fast as they could. We were going to have to fight them to even get out.

More of the humans stared at us, but they had no idea what was going on, and they looked at the staff to come over and sort us out. While three of my party hurried out to the cars, I saw what looked like the manager come over to us.

"Okay. We need to keep these people safe as best we can," I said quietly before he reached us. He tried to smile as I deliberately met his gaze.

"Could we get the bill, please?" I smiled and tried to act as if he had nothing to worry about because we were going to go quietly.

"Of course you can, ma'am. Was everything all right

with your food?" He glanced nervously at me and the group around me. They were all grabbing rucksacks and belongings in what looked like a hurry and leaving whatever was left.

"It was great. We just need to deal with something suddenly..." I had no idea what to say.

How did I tell an entire group of humans that their lives were in danger from a group of demons of the nightmares they tried to forget? How did I warn these people in any way that didn't make them think I was crazy?

Not sure what else to do, I took out my card, handed it to Ben, and closed my eyes to focus on what I felt coming. Taking several deep breaths and ignoring what I was sure were the stares of everyone in the room, I mapped out the enemy in my head.

I noticed the familiar feel of Fintar first. The handler was here and coming closer with an army of minions. Of the demons he commanded, I felt at least five of them on this side of the building, and they were moving fast. I didn't think we'd be able to get three cars out of here and away before they hit.

But worse than that was the six or so shadow catchers I felt coming from the back of the building. I was afraid humans were going to get hurt if we didn't do something fast.

As I opened my eyes, I looked at my mother and saw the understanding on her face.

"I'll take the rear with the spare dragons. I've defended humans before. You take this front lot and go after that handler," she said before I could process what to ask of her.

I blinked at the decisiveness in her voice and the confidence in both of us.

As everyone came back, we handed out the shields and anything else we thought we could use to help us defend. I reached for the collective power of the group and raised my own sword and shield. It was time to fight.

CHAPTER TWENTY-TWO

It didn't take long for two groups to form inside the restaurant. There were eleven of us, and I wished we had a second yellow dragon. I tried to assign Flick to my mother's group, but both of them refused.

"His place is by your side, and I just need to hold. You need to attack." My mother looked me dead in the eyes, and Flick folded his arms.

"Okay, but then Jace and Capricia are going with you. You need their ability to hold a line. Neritas, Flick, Ben, Tim, and Harriet can come with me and help me attack this group."

"You've definitely got the bloodthirsty, spry lot of the bunch," Capricia responded. She didn't look entirely happy about being assigned to a group that didn't contain any of her city's citizens.

Whether I'd made the right choices or not, we had no more time to think about it, and people were reacting to us like we were going to start a fight. The manager came back with the check, and it was clear he wanted us to leave his establishment.

Ben moved to intercept him as another waiter arrived to help herd us out the door. I ignored them this time and made sure all the shields were charged. As my mother revealed a sword, relief rushed through me. It was easier to trust her skills seeing her in action, but I knew we needed to find more equipment if this sort of thing was going to continue.

Screams from outside stopped everyone in their tracks.

"They're here," I said, nodding to my mother as she encouraged her group toward the back of the restaurant.

"Not more of you. I think I'm going to have to ask you to leave." The manager tried to make himself look bigger while the waiter processed the payment as quickly as he could.

"Not more of us. What's hunting us. Trust me. You don't want us to leave. You want us to stay and keep you alive." I turned my back on him and looked at the group I had. Tim held up his shield and moved to my side. Neritas had one of the large serving trays in his hand, holding it by the edge over his body. I shrugged and charged it up for him.

"Please put that down," the manager said, pointing at the tray. "I don't want to have to call the police."

"You can call them if you want, but there's nothing they'll be able to do. Their bullets are just going to piss off what's coming, and everyone here will end up dead. If you give it another minute, you'll understand everything I'm telling you."

Without giving the manager a chance to respond, but

noticing that Ben had my credit card back, I walked toward the front door. My entire team got into position.

I felt the connection to my mother and was grateful for it. It would help me know that she was okay. Right now, I felt her moving away from me, moving past other customers. Looking out at the parking lot, I opted to head out there and meet the shadow catchers in the open before they could get much closer.

"Stay close. This could get rough. I don't need any of you touching me, but it will help me keep the shields charged and you safe."

No one replied, but I assumed they had heard me. At the same time, I had an idea of how to protect everyone inside the restaurant as more screams came from ahead and people ran in our direction.

"Get inside," I yelled and touched the wall of the building. Drawing on the magic in the sword and from my friends, I charged the entire restaurant front, making it dangerous to any shadow catcher that got too close.

With everything I'd learned while connected to the dais and the efficiency of the sword in storing the magic and giving it back to me in combined form, it didn't take too much energy, and it meant I could easily walk forward and do the same to the cars in the parking lot until we had a long row of them we could also use as shields.

By the time I'd done that, the humans running past could see me with the glowing sword and shield as I marched forward and seemed to accept that I was there to defend them.

I caught sight of someone pulling out a phone to film me, but I had no way of stopping that. The handler was sending shadow catchers after me in broad daylight, and I had to defend people. If that meant someone made a video and posted it on social media, I couldn't do anything about it.

Taking a few more steps forward, I felt toward the handler. I needed to get to him and keep the pressure on him, but the shadow catchers were coming up fast.

Moving along the row of cars and out in front of them, I charged a few more of the parked cars in his direction and headed toward the first creature I saw. It was still several yards away from the others, scaring more humans my way, so I rushed it, hearing rather than seeing my friends follow after me.

I stabbed at it, moving fast and getting the first hit in a fraction before its beak collided with the shield. In the light of day, they were more transparent than ever and hard to see.

As the monster cried out in pain loud enough to make my ears hurt, I had to dodge its tail and body as it swung them toward me.

The attack took me by surprise and unbalanced me, but Ben caught me and pushed me back upright as Neritas blocked another beak attack. The creature squealed again but left a dent in the tray and stole its charge.

"Touch it to my skin," I yelled as I stabbed the shadow catcher again and cut another hole in its torso.

"Problem over here," Tim called as Neritas did as I said so that I could charge up his makeshift shield.

I glanced Tim's way to see the next shadow catcher arrive. It shrieked in anticipation of an attack, and more of the humans behind us cried out in terror.

"Get back near me." I fell back a few paces as everyone shrank back between the two cars I'd charged, and Tim, Neritas, and I held the gap with our shields almost entirely touching.

It gave the demon I'd been fighting a chance to recover, but it also meant that we could protect more people and not get hurt.

As the shadow catchers followed and attacked both my companions again, I felt Flick reach over and add electricity to the cars on either side. I stabbed right and then left.

The first shadow catcher was vaporized, easing the pressure on my mind as the second flailed into the car. It was jolted by the charge. Interestingly, the electricity seemed to paralyze it for a few seconds.

I stabbed it again and shoved it back from the car before adding a charge. Before I could speak, Flick added his power, too, making it crackle again. Grateful that he had done so without me needing to ask, I tried to attack again. The shadow catcher fell back, wounded and moving strangely but still alive.

I hesitated, not sure if I should go after it, but I noticed two more of the monsters had converged on my position.

To my horror, they weren't heading straight for me but were chasing down a woman. I panicked, not sure I could get there in time to save her, but sure I needed to try.

Careful to avoid the car, I ran around the front of it again and charged at the wounded shadow catcher. I didn't try to avoid it but slammed into it with both sword and shield, focusing on powering both up.

"Get to the woman and help her this way," I yelled to Neritas and Tim as I kept the shadow catcher busy.

If Fintar had been controlling it, he seemed to abandon the monster to his fight now. My powerful shield and the weight of my body burned into it as I stabbed and twisted the blade again and again. It vaporized, and I almost fell forward.

As soon as it was gone, I ran on, some more of my group with me. I was only twenty meters from my friends and the woman they had managed to reach and shield, but they had both already taken a hit, and the charge in their shields had dissipated.

"I'm coming," I yelled, not sure what else to do to get their attention and encourage them to fall back.

My call brought the frightened woman to her senses, and instead of cowering behind Neritas and staying out of the way, she ran back toward us. Ben waved her through a gap in the cars and ordered her into the restaurant as I hurried forward and stabbed at the nearest shadow catcher just as it slammed its beak into the dragon-built shield Tim had again.

Without my magic, it was decaying, but it showed no other signs of attack, Tim managing to harden it a little. I sliced into the shadow catcher so far that as it shrieked and tried to pull away, its tail swung around and caught me in the side.

I let out a gasp of pain and flung myself to the side and behind Tim. It had only been a brief touch, but it had already decayed a hole in my jeans and tainted my skin underneath. The smell was so bad I gagged, but I pulled magic into me to take away the pain and stop the wound from getting any worse.

Both shadow catchers charged at me as if they sensed my weakness. I rolled as everyone else backed away, and our group was briefly in disarray. I scrambled to my feet by the front of a car as its hood took another strike meant for me. Still not fully upright, I drove my sword upward into the underneath of the same demon.

It writhed and pulled itself backward, but I didn't get any respite as the next one appeared and lunged for me.

Not sure what else to do, I charged the car, using magic from the sword as I pulled backward and scrambled up onto the hood. The shadow catcher lashed out at me and slammed its beak down into it. It shuddered in pain, but the beak still went through the hood and broke something underneath.

Decay started to spread through the vehicle. Metal rusted and grew older before my eyes, paint flaked off, and rubber fell apart.

I backed onto the roof, fueling the car with magic, but the shadow catchers were instructed to pull away by their handler, and I had a moment to look around and survey the battle.

My mother was still somewhere inside the building, and now more shadow catchers were on her side than mine. More were coming this way, though, from farther out. It was as if someone had flooded this place with them, and we were going to be swamped if we weren't careful.

The humans were now mostly safe inside, and the rest were trying to get safe while I kept the nearest demons busy.

Two shadow catchers were injured nearby, and a third, fresh one, was coming in close. My team was regrouping, although their shields had taken a huge hit and had decayed.

My companions came around behind me and formed up around the cars as I continued to back down the length of the car and keep it charged. The shadow catchers came, one down each side, being careful not to touch anything. I quickly rethought my strategy.

I jumped off the car onto the most wounded monster and slashed downward while positioning the shield so it would hit the creature in front of my feet.

My shield hit it, making it reel back and throw its head up to lash back. As I sliced down with the blade, I severed its head, and it vaporized. I turned back to the car, hauled myself back up, and jumped down on the other side of the second demon as the creature went for Tim again.

Tim blocked the beak strike with an uncharged shield. It held, only taking a little more decay and starting to get a flaky appearance. I stabbed the creature in the back and hacked and slashed as it writhed between us, and Tim pushed back and dodged the tail and head as they swung about.

Within a few more seconds, it was also vaporized. The third was still far enough away that I had a little time to focus elsewhere. I rushed toward my group and recharged their shields. As soon as I was beside them, I felt for the next shadow catchers. I considered going after Fintar now that only one of his minions was between me and him, but I couldn't see him, only feel his presence, and lots more monsters were coming.

Instead, I ran with my group to attack the final demon

nearby, aware it was going to get to us before I could do much more anyway. This one had been sucking up water as it came closer, and it moved faster, dodging my first two attacks and getting a swipe at me that passed so close to an arm it frayed more of my clothes and caught the skin underneath.

It stung less than the wound I'd taken to the leg, but my mind automatically took away the pain and got me moving again. I stabbed and hacked and slashed as Neritas and Tim shoved the charged metal at it and helped herd it where I needed it. Working as a team again, all of us now well practiced, we quickly sent this one back to the underworld as well.

I went to get on top of a car again to look out around the parking lot or find Fintar, but I felt so many of the demons that I hesitated. At least another ten were coming out this side, and I could still feel four around the back of the restaurant, trying to make their way inside. On top of that, several more approached on the other side.

As sirens sounded and cop cars started to arrive, Neritas and Ben encouraged me to fall back inside the building. Maybe having the cops here and having lost several shadow catchers already would dissuade Fintar from continuing his attack.

And if that didn't work, I was going to have to work out how to hold a line while I picked off the monsters one by one. That wasn't going to be easy outdoors.

We slipped inside to find the humans huddled in the middle of the restaurant to one side, the manager trying to get everyone to sit down calmly. A few braver humans were filming us and had obviously been at the windows, including the waiter who had served us breakfast.

When the manager spotted us, he pointed to my mother and her smaller team as they tried to protect a back area where the monsters had already partially broken through the building and were trying to get in. She was holding them back, but barely.

I rushed to help her, not wanting her to get hurt but afraid I wouldn't get there in time to see her safely through. This was beginning to feel like an impossible fight. There were just too many monsters.

CHAPTER TWENTY-THREE

Somehow, I ran faster than I ever had, not sure my companions could keep up but not caring right now. All I could think about was getting to my mom to help her.

I stabbed at a shadow catcher right before it could lash out at her. It had been working its way around to the side of her group while Capricia was busy defending against another.

The screech it gave made people behind me squeal, something that wasn't entirely helpful, but I had to focus. The demon came at me next as Neritas and Tim joined Capricia. It helped us drive them back so our groups could merge, but there were still four demons in a small space, and they were angry.

I dodged an attack and hit the monster with my shield, pushing it back and stepping forward. They weren't coming in here, and they weren't hurting anyone I cared about.

They were stronger than I expected, however, and I found I was soon pushed back. I slipped on the smooth floor until my leg hit a chair, the crossbar catching me right where I had been hurt.

Grunting in pain, I stabbed and charged whatever I could around me, making it glow a little to make it more obvious what I'd hit. Ben caught on and picked up the chair before driving its legs into the side of the shadow catcher with all his weight and a battle cry that made shivers run up my spine.

My hurt turned to satisfaction as the demon vaporized. Another one dealt with.

I moved on to another one, but Tim beat me to it and hurled some charged cutlery at it. It must have already been hurt, because it was enough damage to finish the creature off entirely. I stabbed through the puff of air and straight into the next one, and a counterthrust from my mother finished that one off.

The fourth and final monster tried to pull back, but it was hit with several charged objects and stabbed repeatedly by two swords, all of us yelling battle cries.

When it was dead and we stopped, every one of us was panting, and I could see the tiredness. For a fraction of a second, there was only silence, then the humans in the room cheered and celebrated.

I walked toward them along with everyone else, but when they all tried to rush over to us, I put my hand up and shook my head.

"There's more coming. That was just the first wave," I said.

As if to emphasize my words, shots were fired from somewhere outside the front of the restaurant. It seemed the cops had arrived and were finding that their weapons were useless.

"How many more are there?" Ben asked me when he saw the look that passed between me and my mother.

"Twenty, maybe more." Sienna didn't hesitate to deliver the bad news. My entire group faltered and looked at us.

"We need to keep everyone safe and do the best we can," I replied. "If we hold out long enough, the rest will give up. We've already defeated eleven of them."

I did my best to sound as if there was no problem with anything I'd said, but I saw that the shields my companions carried were already breaking. Their trays were gone, and several of us were injured already. Another twenty at once wasn't going to be anywhere near as easy, and we were already partially spent.

"Charge the building," Mother told me, her tiredness showing.

"I'll get that door blocked off again," Neritas said, gesturing for Flick to help him use a table and get it propped up.

The staff and some of the humans inside the building helped. The manager had them moving tables and propping them up against windows and all the openings but the front door.

I didn't let them block that off. With the cops arriving, there were more humans to protect, and we were going to need a way to punch out if we couldn't hold the building.

While my group worked, I charged what I could. One of the waitresses brought out all the trays she could find and a cutlery tray full of knives and forks. I grinned at her quick thinking and observance of our strategy.

"Could you charge the bullets they're wasting out there?" Tim asked.

I blinked, not having considered something like that, but he was right. If I charged the bullets in all the cops' guns, they would actually do some damage and might help us defeat a few more of these monsters.

"Okay, I need a team," I called to the dragons in the room as I went to the door.

The manager looked over at me with fear in his eyes.

"I'll be back, and hopefully with some backup. Get everyone behind as many circles of chairs as you can, with legs facing out like a barricade. My mother will charge it all up so it hurts these things."

If the manager didn't understand any of my words or what they meant exactly, he opted to accept them anyway and gave me a sort of salute. It made me grateful. There was something about the human race that a lot of the dragons in the city didn't seem to appreciate. If they were threatened but knew they could do something about it, they opted to help and grew more determined.

Nothing seemed to crush the human spirit and its capacity for hope and facing a challenge.

I rushed outside and toward the line of cops. As soon as one of them spotted me, they tried to wave me back and away, but I raised the sword and shield and made them glow.

"Your bullets aren't working, are they?" I yelled at the top of my voice.

Some of them glanced my way, but none of them seemed to know how to respond, with the exception of a cop near the back who seemed to be barking orders and trying to get everyone to work together and take up defensive positions.

"Are you telling me that you know something about these creatures?" he asked. His round face was stern, but his brown eyes fixed on me with curiosity.

I nodded as he took in my appearance. His attention lingered on my wounds and my strange shield and sword. Then he took in the group with me.

I took a stab at explaining it. "We can fight them together, but you need me to charge your weapons to make them hurt those things.

Although he raised an eyebrow, he held up his gun. I reached out and connected to it, infusing the bullets. To make it look like I'd actually done something, I made the weapon glow slightly too.

"Now shoot one," I told him as I pulled my hand back and watched his reaction to holding a gun that was now lit up.

He looked for the nearest shadow catcher, in the row of them now halfway across the parking lot and coming in fast. When he fired and the creature wailed and flinched, the other cops cheered.

Shooting again, he focused on the same one until he'd emptied his gun. The last bullet vaporized it, but it also used up more precious seconds.

"I can charge the rest, but I need time, and there's a restaurant full of people these things are aiming for," I said, waving for him and his team to join me.

Thankfully, they had got their spare ammo ready and weapons out for me to charge. We finished quickly and formed back up as one group, then headed back to the only building we could easily defend. I stood by the door, finding all the dragons there with charged shields of one makeshift sort or another. The cops ran in behind, and I took up position over them as the first shadow catchers reached the line of cars right in front.

Fear and anticipation made me shake slightly. I could still feel the handler somewhere nearby, and I knew that we had to survive until I could stop him.

As more monsters approached from the other side, I sent more dragons inside with my mother, and I planted myself firmly in the doorway. I needed to hold them off for as long as possible. At the same time, a single cop appeared by my side with a bag of ammo and guns. I lowered my shield as Neritas and Flick covered me and the dragons hurled cutlery into the first wave of monsters.

Plunging my hand into the weaponry, I drew on the magic in the sword to charge the projectiles and make them all glow a little. When I was done, I nodded at him, and he rushed back to his team to hand it back out.

I grabbed the shield again just in time to step forward and block the first attack. It hit me hard. My body hadn't been quite ready for it, but Tim slammed his shield into it at the same time and used his strength to help shove it back. I noticed he also had a large kitchen knife, and I reached for it with my mind, charging it up for him and doing what I could to keep connected to it.

As more and more of the monsters arrived, it was clear we wouldn't be able to keep holding the door like this. Not without some serious help. No sooner had I thought this than one of the shadow catchers broke a windowpane on the restaurant front. Someone squealed, but the sound was followed by gunfire and the pained cries of shadow catchers being wounded.

It gave me a confidence boost. I wasn't alone, and the demons had probably never faced anything quite like this. It was one thing to make a dragon feel pressured, but ten cops with guns and training—that was another matter entirely. Even if the cops had never faced anything quite like this, they'd been taught to shoot at a threat and ask questions later.

Despite their aid, we were slowly driven back by the sheer weight and strength of the creatures, along with their more reckless approach to fighting. Fintar used them as if they were expendable to push his advantage while he had it, and we had no choice but to try to keep all damage from happening.

Mother was forced away from the fire exit at the back of the building with her smaller team, and the cops were focused in my direction. I had to go inside and help her. We needed to fall back and form a new perimeter again.

"Get all the humans in the kitchen," I yelled as I backed up, and someone brought a table, flipping it onto its side and shoving it over the door, blocking us all inside temporarily. It wasn't part of the plan I'd agreed to—now we had no way out, but I could already see that another table touching the front of the building was losing integrity. The barrier wasn't going to hold much longer anyway.

I felt fewer monsters, but still far too many for me to try anything other than facing them one at a time. As I rushed to help my mother again, shadow catchers broke through at the fire exit once more, and I noticed water was coming across the floor from the kitchen and frowned. They were trying to make themselves stronger and use the fluid around them to heal.

Growling, I threw myself at the nearest shadow catcher, realizing I was going to need to be a little less cautious and aware that this battle was being filmed and cops were now involved.

I worked with Jace to drive another back and pin it down so Capricia could also drive a charged kitchen knife into it and cut its head off. It vaporized, and we almost collapsed into it.

Before I could find another target, I heard my mother cry out and felt a strange pain across the bond and connection we had. I yelled in anger as I spotted the shadow catcher with a beak buried in her shoulder.

Springing up and over a chair someone had been using as a barrier, I threw myself at the shadow catcher. Anger lent me speed and strength, and I drew on the magic of all the dragons around me to go faster until I threw myself at the demon hurting my mother.

Hacking and slashing and pouring magic into my body, I growled and fought, not even feeling the pain when it caught me until it also died. Reijo wrapped an arm around Sienna and helped her back up, and Neritas and Ben moved in front of her, holding fresh shield trays.

"Fall back. To the kitchen," I called when I noticed everyone else was now clear. My voice was getting hoarse. I reached down to charge every inch of the floor, drawing on the sword again, but it emptied before I could do more than push the shadow catchers back a few yards.

Flick grabbed one of my shoulders as Jace wrapped an

arm around my waist, and they pulled me back from the fray. I let them take me back at first, feeling in my mind for what I was facing and how my mom was doing.

We'd killed another three shadow catchers between us, but more than ten still remained, and I had no idea how we were going to survive this when my mother was injured and the cops were running out of bullets. I was the only one who could charge anything, and we had few weapons left.

Somehow, I had to hold the line, however. I couldn't let Fintar win. Not when I'd just found my family and gained the responsibility of saving the entire world.

CHAPTER TWENTY-FOUR

Getting everyone inside the kitchen bought us some time as I charged the walls and drew on the power of the dragons around me to refill my sword and shield. I then charged a counter covered in kitchen utensils and pots and pans. This was all we had left, and we would have to make it count.

As the shadow catchers gathered along the other side of the wall, I knew they were going to try to push through, and there was a chance they were going to bring the roof down on us, so I kept my hand on this side and tried to keep it charged. I was aware that everyone was getting tired, however, and this only worked so well.

The determined shadow catchers still decimated the wall in several places, and a couple of them sacrificed themselves to break it down and rot it through. Once more, I was forced to pull back. I stabbed the face of a demon as it broke through right before I fell into the line of dragons still standing. Behind them were the cops, all of them holding guns with the last few bullets they had.

As a line of shadow catchers broke through, our side let loose our charged projectiles. I only waited a few seconds to see where the most damage was done to make the best use of my powers, and then I hurled myself into the fight again.

My shield blow and stab were enough to dispatch a single monster, but it revealed another behind it.

I ducked back and to one side as Neritas leaned over me and caught the descending beak on the edge of a frying pan. It made a dull *thunk* and stuck for a moment, giving me a chance to recover and stab upward into the creature and drive it back for him. Another creature came in from our right.

Neritas shifted back, and the monster caught his arm and made him hiss as I darted the other way, suddenly cut off and surrounded.

I brought myself into a low half crouch, spun on the ball of one foot, and held my shield and sword arm out as firmly as I could.

I smacked into monsters, cutting up any part of them that got too close. I kept going until I was dizzy, and a couple of them became nothing but tainted air.

Neritas, Flick, and Ben pushed through to me, shoving the reeling demon between us to one side and finishing it off with a skillet my mother must have powered up for them. I stumbled back into the group as I took another hit to my sword arm and screeched in pain.

Capricia and Jace came up on that side and threw a large bag of glowing flour at the creature, pushing it back and giving me more room again. My vision didn't clear as I grew less dizzy, making me sure that I'd pushed too hard and was draining my magic, which meant I'd drawn on the others too much as well.

"We need help," I said, looking for Jace to see if she could call in any fresh dragons like she had done the last time.

"They're on their way, but these things have caught us out in the middle of nowhere useful. We need to hold on longer."

I exhaled, not sure how to buy us more time when we were all so drained already. The creatures kept coming, and there were still so many of them.

My mind felt less pressured, but I felt Fintar finally moving and even more of the demonic creatures coming in another wave, although this one felt smaller again. Was he finally running out of minions?

"The handler is coming," I added and stabbed at another of the demons.

They all pulled back for a moment as if they sensed our weakness and were waiting to make the final strike. I got back in line with all the dragons around me, and my mom stood and tried to join us.

"Use my magic, even if I can't grip a sword right now," she whispered.

I wanted to refuse, but I knew we were going to need it.

"Charge yourself and go get that son of a bitch. Go show him that the power of all the dragon kings and queens flows in you now. You can draw on more than you know and fight even harder than this."

I closed my eyes for half a second to feel all the connections I held. Somehow, I had to keep everyone here safe when I went after Fintar, but it was going to take everything I had left.

Drawing on the magic in my shield and sword, I charged everything around me I could connect to and reach, making all the improvised weapons and shields glow deadly again, and then I pushed it out on the floor and charged forward.

Raising my sword, I yelled and ran, hurtling through the shadow catchers in the way and hitting them as hard as I could.

Still pumping magic into anything close, I felt Neritas, Flick, Ben, Jace, and Capricia come with me, adding their cries to mine. They used shields and weapons as well, and several more monsters died under our onslaught.

As we reached what had been the kitchen wall, we had to break our triangle a little as some of the decayed remains were still there and blocking our path, but we formed up swiftly on the other side.

I didn't have to look far for Fintar. The handler was striding through the warped door in his demonic form, with three more shadow catchers flanking him.

Not giving him time to process what was going on, I rushed them all, still charging everything as I went. It was draining the last of my magic, but I didn't stop or hesitate. This could only go one way. It was time to throw everything I had at this fight.

Fintar had just enough time to bring up a shield and weapon of his own. They were both wreathed in a strange, dark, fog-like substance that moved with them and left a trail that made me think of a cross between black smoke and fire. I blocked the sword swipe with my shield and stabbed at him.

He staggered back, my charge forceful enough to throw him off balance despite the counterattack. I ignored the shadow catchers, hoping the dragons with me could keep them at bay as I kept everything they carried charged. It was a strange feeling to be connected to so much at once and pumping out so much magic, but I didn't hesitate.

As my body moved with instinct I shouldn't have had, I blocked attack after attack and hit out at the handler again and again. He parried well, his limbs moving faster than I could process sometimes. Slowly he was pushing me back, the strain of the fight and all the magic use becoming too much on me.

I panted, silent now and unable to keep yelling, but I couldn't give up. Still standing, I tried to find a way past his defenses, but more demons were still coming in, and they were moving fast. If this didn't end soon, we were going to be overrun.

Fintar seemed to sense this and pushed harder, making me feel even more pressed. Panic rose in me, but I pushed it away, finding it didn't feel like a new emotion anymore. A brief flash of memory that wasn't mine let me know that one of my ancestors had been in this situation before.

Channeling the fire my companions had found inside themselves and feeling the power course through me again, I raised my head, and the sword became lighter in my hand as my limbs moved with new strength. I caught his shield with mine as I danced to one side of him and spun him. He wobbled when I lowered the shield slightly and stabbed over the top of it.

My blade caught his arm and cut into it, the strange shadow parting as my blade sliced through. He let out a screech that sounded like some demonic, distorted dragon cry and tried to slash back. Bringing my shield up and out, I turned the blade from me and stabbed underneath it.

I got him in the leg this time, and he finally rushed back, putting distance between us. Feeling a fire continue to burn through my body while it shook with a power I didn't know I had, I strode confidently toward him. Somewhere nearby, a demon vaporized, and Fintar's eyes widened. I felt another pop in my mind when someone vanquished one in the kitchen.

Fintar took one look at me and turned, intending to run for it. I drew on the power I had in the sword one last time and sped after him, using it to make me faster and more powerful.

With all the force I could muster, I hit him. He went sprawling, and I spun myself around, blocking off his escape as he got back to his feet.

"You're not going anywhere," I said, the words coming out as a half-growl.

He snarled in response and lunged at me again. We fought hard, both of us blocking and moving faster than humanly possible. I moved with the experience of someone beyond my years, surprising myself at the skill and ease with which I blocked another side swipe and countered with a stab to his side.

I caught him again, and a tear that didn't quite go away appeared in the shadows. He lurched back, and I pushed on, making my body move forward and drawing on the last of the magic in the sword and shield to deliver another blow that sent both our shields spinning away from us. Then I stabbed and stabbed.

The fourth strike seemed to finish him off.

Before my eyes, he transformed into something else, a set of deep, almost blackened red dragon scales appearing briefly before he shrank into something that was part human and part another creature I didn't recognize. He was bleeding out, dying before my eyes. As he passed from this world, he dropped his sword and fell to the floor.

I stepped back, not sure what to do as all the remaining shadow catchers around us faltered and my own body started to feel the pain and exhaustion.

The shadow catchers outside continued to come toward us, however. They were slower and moving in a more disorganized fashion suddenly, but it was as if they were still on a mission.

The demons in the building recovered as well, both the one out here and the several more in the kitchen. With a trace of magic still in my sword, I stabbed the shadow catcher ahead in the back before I realized I still didn't have my shield.

Thankfully, my blow finished the creature off, and it blew into smoke that the air conditioning sucked upward and out. I hurried toward my shield as some of my companions returned to the kitchen. Neritas came with me and helped me back to my feet when I wobbled getting my shield from the floor where it had fallen.

I noticed Fintar's shield and reached out to it with my mind. It felt strange, but I could connect to it the same way I did my own. I grabbed it, charged it, and offered it to Neritas.

He raised his eyebrows but took it and felt the weight of it.

"This should work better. It feels... like it holds the power, a bit like yours."

I tilted my head to the side, unsure, hoping I hadn't powered up something I shouldn't have and that it wouldn't feed the shadow catchers' power. But there was only one way to find out.

Hearing more shrieks and feeling the commotion in the kitchen, I waved Neritas back that way, and we rushed into the fray once more. I was dizzy and tired, and every limb ached with fatigue, but the humans and dragons were barely holding on, and the final barricade of chairs was barely keeping the shadow catchers at bay.

Now that nothing was controlling them, they were lashing out at random, and attacks from dragons and humans on all sides confused them. I wasn't sure what was best to do first, but I had to buy some more time for everyone to regroup and for me to get back where I could protect the most vulnerable.

"Everyone close your eyes," I yelled.

I made myself bright enough to blind the demons. I heard the shadow catchers shriek and opened my own eyes to rush at the nearest one and stab it. Neritas and I pushed it to the side.

It must have been less injured because it bore the brunt of the attack but writhed in pain when the strange shield Neritas wielded hit it. The charge remained, not needing me to power it up again.

Grateful that one of my friends could defend himself a

little better, I encouraged everyone back to my side, and the dragons formed a protective line across from the humans and my mother, and the now even more injured Harriet. Capricia also stepped back, panting and clearly dizzy. I disconnected from all of them to make sure I couldn't accidentally pull on their power, and I let them rest while I faced the enemy.

With all the commotion, I was sure I'd lost track of how much energy I was pulling from my companions, but I slowed it now, trying not to draw anything I didn't absolutely need to keep us alive.

Almost instantly, they all appeared to breathe easier and stood a little straighter. Guilt filled me at what I'd been costing them and how much I could have hurt them if I'd not been able to defeat Fintar when I had, but I knew I couldn't have pulled on much less. The sword and shield were almost empty of energy already.

I had little left myself, and I felt as if I might be on my last legs. What we needed were fresh dragons. But none of them were here yet, and there were more shadow catchers outside as well as three left in here.

Once, this many monsters would have scared me, but now I looked at them, knowing that all of them were injured, and I knew we could handle it. They came flailing at us, rage for their own survival fueling them so much that they had little sense of self-preservation at this point. I drew on the magic left in the weapon and shield to hurl myself at the nearest one.

It was quick to die, and within two more minutes, I'd finished off the others with help from Jace, Neritas, Flick, and Ben. The rest of the team simply held the line and stopped flailing limbs from hurting the humans that were close by.

"Are there still more?" Reijo asked, looking back at my mom with a glance that spoke of his concern.

"Yes, but they're not organized anymore," I told him. "I killed their handler. We can get my mother to a car and get out of here."

"I can't let you all drive out of here," the cop in charge said, recovering now that no one was in immediate danger. "I'll need statements, and there's all this damage. What you did to the guns. It needs to be—"

"Look." I clapped the guy on the shoulder as I faced him. "We all know that pretty much anyone who hasn't directly witnessed this isn't going to believe it was real. Most people don't want to believe any of this is real, but I'll tell you what has happened here, so you at least know while my friends gather themselves and everything they need and get ready to flee. That's going to have to be enough."

He opened his mouth as if he was going to speak, but the manager came up and shook my other hand.

"You saved all of us. Thank you, thank you."

"Sorry about all the damage," Ben said, taking the manager to one side and giving me one of his subtle nods to let me know he'd handle the manager.

I gave my attention back to the cop as more of them gathered around. I had to assume someone was still filming, and that made me worried about what I said. One thing I had always valued, however, was honesty, so I decided to shoot for that and be vague.

"You're looking at the queen of a race that you all

thought long dead but is not. We've been hiding for millennia, protecting the planet and keeping you all safe from the creatures you saw today. But we've run into a few problems lately, and the safety measures we had in place are weakening. We're dealing with it, but today it spilled out into your part of the world and your day. I'm sorry for that, but with any luck, this is the only time you'll ever see or hear of us or them."

"Race?" he asked, the word coming out of his mouth as if it barely held back a tidal wave of other questions along with it.

"Dragons," I replied. "We can take human form and use magic."

Although I tried to be discrete about it, I wanted the cops to see. I transformed my hand, turning it into a dragon claw and showing my deep red scales for all of them to see. They gasped, and one of them stepped back. A moment later, I appeared entirely human again.

"I have to go now. My mother requires medical aid that you can't provide."

"But I need a statement. You have to do what I say by law." He shook his head and reached out to stop me. "Please don't resist."

"Tell me, sir, do you think a queen outranks a police officer?" I asked as Neritas and Reijo helped my mother out, both of them holding shields and other dragons going with them.

This silenced him, but I could see him wanting to object again. I turned and walked away before he could change his mind and try to make this difficult. I didn't want to have to hurt anyone else.

CHAPTER TWENTY-FIVE

Once I was outside, I saw the shadow catchers still out there and milling around. Some of them came toward us, but a large van also came driving up. I felt the presence of more dragons, and Jace hurried toward it and waved them down.

Other than the few dragons guarding my mother, we all moved toward the van and the shadow catchers. A couple of familiar faces and several I didn't recognize got out and looked at Jace.

"She's in charge. I'll explain later." Jace pointed at me. "She can kill these things if you stick near her and let her use your magic."

I connected to them as she spoke, making it obvious what she was talking about, and then I charged up the shields they were carrying and any of the improvised weapons and shields the others still carried.

"Let's finish this lot off," I added before turning back to the monsters.

One had come close, either picking up on my scent or

all the noise, and I started with that, running at it and blocking its attack before I stabbed right into its center.

Feeling much better now that I could draw on the magic of fresh dragons without feeling too guilty, I felt the aches and pains drop away as I attacked and moved like I had centuries of experience.

Before anyone could help me, I killed the shadow catcher and looked for the next. I heard gasps as the new dragons witnessed a feat they'd never seen before, and Jace laughed.

Now more eager and a little less scared, the newcomers followed me into battle, and we dispatched more of the creatures in quick succession. When the fourth one was sent back to the underworld, it seemed to break something in the others, and they turned and fled.

If I'd not been concerned for my mother, I'd have gone after them and done everything I could to make sure they were never a problem to anyone ever again, but I didn't dare. Instead, I nodded my thanks to Jace and rushed back to Reijo's car.

"How is she?" I asked, nothing else on my mind despite the cops emerging from the restaurant and humans returning to the area to take in all the destruction.

"She'll be okay," Reijo replied for her. "But we could do with getting her to the farmhouse. I've got something you can power there that will help until she can get somewhere safe to rest."

"We'll go to the dragon city with Scarlet after," I heard my mother say from the back of the car.

I nodded, not intending to argue, and aware that

Capricia was standing by impatiently. When she saw my reaction, she exhaled and relaxed a bit more.

"Do you know how many dragon rules we've broken today?" she asked as we walked back toward my own car.

Jace waved her group back to her car and van, but I reached for her.

"Come with us," I said as I stopped her. "At least let me heal Harriet and anyone else who is hurt before you go."

"I can come with you to your mother's, but I think we both know that none of my group should come with you back to the city. We would only hurt your appearance as you inform them of who you are." Jace smiled at me, but she had a sad light in her eyes.

Although I didn't want to admit it, she was right. If I was to win the trust of all the dragons, I had to get them to understand who I was and what I could do for them before I changed everything they held sacred. It would be hard enough to convince some of them that there was a real danger and that they hadn't been taught the truth.

For now, it gave us a course of action, and I let myself be ushered into one of the waiting vehicles. Now up to four, and with seventeen dragons in total, I felt as if I was part of a large, powerful convoy. If we'd had one more red dragon, we would have had three full fighting units, but if my mother was to be believed, there was a good chance that would never be possible.

It made me wonder how I was ever going to continue the red dragon line and protect the world from the demon behind the gate if there were no others. The prospect of having a child with any male red dragon that did exist simply to make sure that the line continued filled me with emotions I didn't want to feel.

Something like that wasn't worth thinking about right now, but I knew that at some point, it would come up. At some point, I would have to consider an heir, just as my mother had ensured my father had one. It seemed that her not being perfectly red had caused issues, though. It was interesting that she could use the red dragon abilities as well as she could, however.

I still had so many questions for my mother. It had made my heart glad to hear her say she was going to come back to the city with me, but it appeared not everyone was happy with the plan we had so far. Capricia and Ben had both been quiet since we had driven off.

Neritas was admiring his new shield, and Flick was checking it out with him and comparing the wounds they had gathered. Both of them had gotten hurt, but nothing that wouldn't heal, although I suspected Neritas was in some pain from the attack he'd taken to the arm. I was feeling dull aches from my own wounds, and they all had a faint aroma of infection and rot.

It was almost sickly sweet but also unpleasant and off somehow. I hoped whatever device Reijo had spoken of could also help the rest of us.

While we drove, we snacked on our provisions and tried to gather our strength. I didn't have much physical energy left or mental energy for talking, but everything seemed to be getting better until several cop cars appeared behind us on the road and joined the end of our convoy. A moment later, I got a message from Jace.

Want me to try and get rid of them?

Her message landed just as Capricia put her foot down a little and tried to encourage Reijo, the front driver in our convoy, to go a little faster.

"It's okay," I said to Capricia and typed the same message to Jace. "Let them follow us. They're not going to shoot at us, and they don't have the sirens or flashing lights on. They'll just want to talk when we stop somewhere."

I wasn't sure how my mother would feel about us leading them to her farmhouse, but if she was coming with me to the city, she wasn't going to need it for a while. She could always stick with me until all this had blown over or been sorted out. Maybe until the cops had realized that no one was going to believe them.

The journey back to the farmhouse felt as if it took a long while despite it being barely over an hour, and I wondered if I could bear the long journey back to the West Coast and LA if it was going to be like this.

Something was up with Capricia, and I was worried about Ben. While we drove and I didn't know what might be wrong, I didn't dare bring it up, especially as neither of them did either.

Thankfully, we soon arrived at the farmhouse, and everyone got out. Reijo and Flick helped my mother as Cios took a team to check everything was safe and that no demons had been here recently.

I went to walk away from the cops, seeing Jace head in that direction, but Capricia grabbed my elbow and held me back from the house.

"This isn't good. We're meant to be keeping our presence a secret from the human world, and I think you should also be downplaying this royal thing. No one in the city is going to like it. No one wants a royal red dragon anymore, and they're not going to like your proof. You need to get the elders on your side first."

There was some merit to Capricia's words, but Neritas came to my other side before she could finish and shook his head.

"There may be some who don't want a queen or any kind of royal, but it's not the elders who get to decide if there is one or not. The citizens of our city deserve the truth. They deserve someone being honest with them from the beginning. She has as much proof as there is ever going to be." Neritas narrowed his eyes and folded his arms across his chest.

"Thank you, both of you, for expressing your opinions," I said. "I will consider both and do what I think is best. Right now, however, I would like to heal those who are hurt and help everyone recover from the fight we've been in. It matters to me more that everyone survives this without unnecessary pain than that I have an exact plan for something that won't happen for another day or two."

Before either of them could respond, I walked into the house and went to look for my mother. I needed to help her and didn't want to think about anything else yet. Both of my friends had a point, but I couldn't let them sway me from what I thought was right.

I didn't have to go far before Reijo appeared. He had an amulet in his hand, a gemstone on a string, and he held it out to me, encouraging me to touch it. I took it and tried to connect my mind to it. It felt strange, unlike the sword and shield. I felt it drawing on my magic, though, and I fed it before heading through to my mother.

She was sitting in the kitchen at the breakfast bar along with Harriet and Tim, who had all been hurt. I called for anyone else to come join us who needed healing and sat down myself.

"This is a little difficult to use," Mom said as I brought it close to her wounded shoulder.

The smell of the rotten flesh the monsters had created made me gag slightly, but I did my best to hide it and focus on the healing device. After taking a deep breath, I closed my eyes and got ready to follow whatever instructions Mom gave me.

As I concentrated, my mind and instincts took over, and I felt the device itself guiding me. It wanted to use the magic to heal, and it didn't want to be used to store magic the way I'd tried. Almost immediately, it got to work, fighting the infection and restoring the cells of the body.

The strange artifact wasn't perfect, but it seemed to work with the body it was healing. It took its time, but the wound grew cleaner before my eyes, and the grimace on my mother's face eased. It didn't heal all the way, but it was as if several days of healing had passed in only a few minutes before the device would do no more.

I brought it to my own skin and the wound aching on my leg. It wasn't as bad as my mother's had been, but it was still deep enough that it had been bleeding, and it looked slightly infected. Again, the artifact kicked in, drawing on my magic only as it needed it and working gently with the body.

My leg warmed as the pain and itching faded, and soon

it was far easier to bear. Before I healed the rest of the smaller injuries I had, I moved on to my friends and made sure all of them were fine. Harriet was the next most hurt, and I was able to take care of the older wound she had too. It was wonderful to know that the device my mother had could harness all our magic to heal everyone.

It took the best part of an hour, but eventually, everyone had been seen to. No one had been unscathed after the battle. The cops stuck around, asking questions that no one wanted to answer, but giving me some grace as they watched me help everyone. When I noticed that three of the eight cops who had followed us were also injured, I got to work healing them and easing their pain.

"Please, miss, can we get a name and some more information? I have to make a report," the cop in charge said as I finished healing everyone. He crouched beside my seat and looked me in the face.

"I get it. I know that you're just trying to understand all this and make everything safe. That you've got a nightmare on your hands explaining it, but if I give you details about me, what will happen?" I asked. "It's very important that nothing is confirmed in the public eye. This needs to be covered up."

"You've seen what's already on social media, right?" one of the others asked. He pulled up a social media site on his phone and showed me the viral video and other snippets that were being shared. It was already being picked up by mainstream media.

"I've already got my boss asking me what the hell happened."

I exhaled as everyone looked at me for answers. This

wasn't something I'd ever thought I'd have to handle. What could be done about this? How could this be explained away?

"Tell them it was a gang fight. Tell them it was terrorists. Tell them it was a gas leak. Whatever you think will satisfy the masses best. But you cannot tell them the truth. I shouldn't have even told the few of you. It breaks all our rules, and it will not gain me any favors with the elders of my city." I looked the cop in the eyes, hoping he'd continue to understand that I was helping him as best I could and that we were both in difficult positions.

"I thought you were the queen."

"I am, but not all of them know that yet."

"We were out here trying to find the proof we need and equip Scarlet for the coming fight," Ben said as he also sat.

"Scarlet?" the cop asked, looking at me.

I nodded, not sure if it was a good idea they knew my name. Neritas and Capricia glared at Ben for giving that much away.

"I'm Scarlet. And I've been living as a human for a very long time. The dragon part of this world isn't ideal, but you've seen what I can do today, and I hope you understand that all I'm trying to do is kill those monsters and stop people from getting hurt."

"It's the only reason I've not arrested you already. If it hadn't been for you, I get the feeling that we'd all be dead."

"And if Scarlet doesn't return to the dragon community and unite them against these things, eventually, everyone will die." Ben got up as if this was the end of the conversation and he was taking charge.

"I'm Bryce. And you have the gratitude of myself and all

of my team in there with you today. But I have one last request to make, and I'll let you walk out of here and get on with your life. Give me some way to contact you. Something that will satisfy my boss that I can reach you if I need to ask you more questions. He'll accept that I haven't just let you go without some confidence that I can make a report and I don't have to chase you or fight you."

I grinned at his oh-so-human logic. He made no request that I answer any more questions, and I could respect the loophole approach. It made my mind up, and I gave him the phone number for the extra phone Jace had given me. It was the least likely to cause a problem, and I knew it wouldn't be able to be traced to anyone. Jace nodded her approval at the idea, though Capricia still stood with folded arms and a frown on her face.

This satisfied the guests, and several of the cops shook my hand and those of others they had fought alongside before heading back out to their cars.

"We should go too," Jace said later. "I need to get back to our folks and let them know the important stuff. They'll want to talk to you as well."

"We'll arrange something," I replied as everyone prepared to leave.

I still had my rucksack, but it was bulkier than it had been with my new possessions inside it—in particular, a crown and several other new objects that could prove who I was. I tucked the healing device inside it, careful not to reveal the crown, then shouldered my pack, and we returned to the cars.

We left the farmhouse and my mother's dwelling of many years. Before long, Cios led the van away, and we became a convoy of two cars. We'd already opted to drive through the night, with Ben taking over for Capricia when she got too tired and my mother also agreeing to drive Reijo's car.

For the first time, I felt as if I was heading home. Back to the city where I belonged. At least for now.

CHAPTER TWENTY-SIX

As we drove along the last section of the road to the city, I tried to wake myself up a bit more. I'd been sleeping, my head resting on Flick's shoulder and Neritas resting on me. The three of us had gotten used to being in close quarters in the back of a car over the last few days and had slept in the best way we could while in such a small space.

Now that I was awake enough to realize how close I was to the city, nerves settled in. I was terrified of what would happen in the next few hours. I was about to claim a throne, and, in truth, I had no idea how to rule. This wasn't something I'd been preparing for my whole life. I had to figure it out as I went.

I didn't have past kings and queens as advisers, and from what my mother had told me, there weren't many people left alive, and even fewer of them in the city, who had been in service to the royal family. The elders had taken over the governing role as best they could in each city, and now the dragons had no central leadership.

Because it had always acted as the seat of power, the

city near LA was the one that ruled over all the others, but I'd learned that there weren't masses of them around the world, and they mostly acted autonomously. For the most part, the dragons were a fractured race, and hiding away in their cities.

This needed to change. But not everyone was going to like that.

I knew that the people with me had different opinions on what I should do and how, and that was enough to make me question myself. I didn't think I could keep them all happy, and it would only be worse with a city full of people, and that didn't take into account the other cities full of dragons that might have a different way of thinking and doing things.

Whatever I did next, all I could focus on was trying my best and hoping that my own conscience could cope with the results. I had nothing else to go on.

It didn't bring me much comfort, however. My mind was far too good at imagining all the possible ways this could go horrendously wrong and all the horrible outcomes I couldn't control.

"It'll be okay," Flick said as he picked up on the way I was shaking. My heart was racing as Capricia turned onto the part of the road that only dragons could find.

To my surprise, I could feel the city beyond, and unlike all the times Ben had driven off the edge of the cliff and I had feared us taking a long dive into the water, this time, I knew it was the right direction and that the city lay beyond. Every dragon there was like a tiny beacon that let me sense the entire city.

I tried not to be distracted by it as the car went through

the shield and we could suddenly see the city and everyone inside anyway. Looking back, I made sure Reijo had managed to follow okay and that he and Mother were safely on this side of it.

It had been tempting to ride with them when I got back, but everyone had agreed it was better for me to come back with the companions I had left with, still one of them.

I'd opted to get out carrying the sword and shield Neritas had taken for me and not hide that they were mine. That much was all they knew of what I planned to do, and until recently, it was all I had been able to decide upon for sure. I had no more time to change my mind now, though. I had to plow onward with my latest decision.

As Capricia pulled to a stop, Neritas, Flick, and Ben all looked at me to check I was ready.

"Let's do this," I said.

Moving as one, the three of them got out of the car at once, and by the time Reijo had pulled up and parked near us, several dragons were flying down and landing to greet us. I noticed Brenta from the elders' council again, as well as Tiffany and other dragons who were curious.

I let Capricia get out while I decided which way to get out of the back. Something about Neritas and his words in support of me being his queen, along with Ben being on that side of the car, made me head that way.

Neritas reached back to help me get out. As he shut the car door behind me, a hush spread over the city.

My mother and Reijo had gotten out of their car, and Mom was closer and smiling at me. Before I could do more than move closer, Neritas got down on one knee and bowed in front of me, and then Flick and Ben did the same.

I could barely breathe, let alone speak, as Reijo and my mother also followed suit.

"The queen has returned. All hail the queen," Neritas called as he looked back up at me.

This wasn't what I'd had in mind, but Ben called it next, and then all my companions joined in with him.

Tiffany ran up, a look of delight shining in her eyes, and she bowed. Her actions started a trickle of similar reactions, and more of the dragons landed and took human form to do the same. Jared was one of the first few to do so, as well as some of my other teachers and classmates.

I noticed that not everyone did. Brenta didn't move or acknowledge what was happening. I now had to work with what I had, not sure whether to be angry at Neritas for taking the decision out of my hands or grateful that whatever happened now, I wouldn't blame myself if the city reacted badly. I walked toward Brenta.

When I finally moved, my companions got back to their feet and fell in behind me, my mother and Ben taking up positions behind each of my shoulders.

Brenta stiffened as I drew closer, her eyes not leaving my face.

"I would speak to the elders. We'll convene them right away and hold an open session for the city to hear."

"And who is it that thinks they have the authority to command the elders to appear before them?" she asked with ice in her tone.

For a moment, I didn't respond, knowing that a lot of people were listening.

"I do. Scarlet, a pure red dragon, daughter of King

Kauis and queen of the dragons. The elders serve the throne as I do, and there is much to discuss."

She blinked, her composure slipping for a fraction of a second. She hadn't expected me to be so bold, and even I was a little surprised by how confident I sounded. I felt anything but confident on the inside.

After glancing at my mother with no curiosity or desire to get to know her, Brenta turned and led the way.

I focused on my breathing and simply walking without making an idiot of myself as we made our way to the central tower of the city. Although Brenta went to climb up it, I changed my mind at the last minute and instead leaped into the air and turned into a dragon.

Flying up, I stretched my wings and enjoyed the few seconds of airtime it took to get all the way to the top of the tower. My companions followed me without much effort.

As I landed on the open part of the elders' tower at the top, I transformed back into a human. For the first time ever, I managed to time it perfectly, feeling the knowledge of all the dragons before me helping with that too. I was a bit more precise and confident, my body and mind able to do these things as if they were practiced enough now.

I waited for everyone else to land, noticing that it wasn't just my companions and Brenta who had followed. Many of the dragons in the city were heading this way, a ripple of knowledge and my claim spreading as they all talked to each other.

Neritas had made sure that the entire city knew who I was claiming to be, and they knew I intended to tell the elders I was in charge and prove my claim.

As my mother and Ben landed beside me, they both gave my hands a squeeze. Brenta landed next, and then Neritas and Flick. When I looked his way, Neritas had the good grace to at least avoid my gaze and look a little ashamed of what he'd done and the drama he had caused. It didn't matter now. I couldn't change what had happened.

Brenta glared at me as she strode beside me toward the entrance to the chamber. I saw the rest of the elders inside, another dragon having landed and already begun telling them what had happened.

I motioned for her to lead the way inside, something that only made her angrier, but I couldn't fix that either. I had a feeling that no matter what was said, she would oppose me. She had taken a dislike to me from the beginning.

As I walked in behind her, all my companions followed, and the informant of the elders fell quiet as they all looked my way.

Trying not to show the fear I felt, I strode to the center of the room, knowing that every lie said in there could be picked up on. I found there was an artifact in the center of the room I could now sense. It held a connection to each of the elders, but it reached for my mind as well.

The strange feeling that had come over me both of the previous times that I had stood in the chamber was now far more understandable. An artifact I didn't understand had been offering me a connection of sorts.

I reached for it now, but I kept the interaction with it to nothing more than letting it know I was there. Until I understood it a little better, I didn't want to use it and possibly alert the rest of the room to my new ability to connect to it.

No one spoke as the elders got into place, moving to their seats on the far wall, a semi-circle of judgment and inquiry. I glanced back to see everyone who had arrived with me and plenty of other dragons too. Some of them moved to step inside, but the guards blocked their way.

"No, let them in. Let them all in if they wish," I said loud enough that everyone would hear me.

There were a few gasps, and the guards blinked in shock.

"This is the elders' chamber. We will decide if they come in or not. Shut the doors," Brenta commanded from her seat in the middle.

As she spoke, I felt a ripple from the artifact and wondered if it was trying to tell me something.

"No." I added more command to my voice. "I have called for a public audience with the elders. Let them in."

"You don't have the authority to make that request." Brenta raised her hand to have the guards do as she commanded, and I felt a definite ripple in the room as if she had lied and the artifact was letting me know.

"Yes. I do. You've just lied. And as the chamber lets you know when someone makes a false claim, I can feel the false claim you've made."

As soon as I uttered the words, I noticed the other elders reach mentally into the artifact, their connections growing deeper.

"Is it true? You can feel the truth of another's words?" the kindlier elder asked of me.

"Yes. I can connect to the same artifact that you can and

feel the same information you do. It was as if there was a spare connection just waiting for me to take it."

More gasps from the other dragons, including some of the ones by the door.

"She speaks the truth," another of the elders declared.

No one spoke after this. Brenta looked around at the dragons that, until now, had been entirely in charge of the city and then back to me.

"If you are truly who you say you are, then where is your proof?" Brenta asked eventually.

"I found my mother."

Sienna stepped forward as I spoke.

"My daughter speaks the truth. She is older than she first appeared and older than Anthony and Ben believed. I kept her hidden for the first six years of her life and have kept her heritage a secret until she could come and find me. It was her father's wish that she grow up in the human world and be safe until she was ready."

"And how do we know that you are not mistaken?"

"Brenta, she is speaking in the chamber. We would know if she was lying."

"But we don't know if this is the heir without Kauis here himself to tell us for sure. There is more to becoming the queen of the dragons than simply declaring it." Brenta sounded like a cross schoolteacher correcting a child and not happy about having to do so.

I opened my mouth to say that I would be willing to go through whatever process was necessary when Ben stepped forward.

"All the required elements have already been fulfilled. Scarlet has stood on the pinnacle before her ancestors on the island of Kilnar. She was found worthy and returns with the power of her father and the royal line inside her already."

The silence that followed this statement was so complete that I was sure if I exhaled, everyone would hear it. I hadn't realized the importance of what had happened until this moment.

"There is nothing more to debate or decide," Neritas declared as he also came up beside my mother and me on the other side. "You have more than one witness before you, and she has declared her intention herself. She is our queen. Unless any of you intend to challenge her for her right to the throne, you must recognize her."

"Thank you, Neritas. I'm sure the elders don't need you to tell us what the correct process is," Brenta snapped. She didn't look at him as she spoke.

I stepped forward again and walked almost all the way up to her.

"I'm pretty sure that you don't like me, but the only reason I am standing before you now and claiming this throne is because you all need me to. Evil is growing more powerful. The gate is weakening, and I have been given the strength and knowledge to help the dragons come together and stop it once more. It is my duty, and I'm the only one who can do it. I have no desire to subvert the day-to-day running of this city or upset any of the roles you play in this city's governance and among dragons everywhere. You are not being fired or replaced, nor is your task being changed. I am going to have plenty to focus on."

"The gate is weakening? This isn't possible. It is known that the dragons power it," one of the elders said.

"Yes," I replied. "Dragons do power it, but not in the way taught in the city."

I walked over to the elder and pulled out my phone to show some of the proof I had that the evil was spreading and things weren't as they seemed. Over the next few minutes, I provided an overview of everything I had been up to and filled them all in on the handler I had fought.

Now and then, Ben and Sienna joined me in explaining what had happened. I acted as calmly as I could while also making it clear that I had been hunted for a reason by the evil.

While we talked, many of the city dragons listened, some of them in the chamber with us, but even more on the balcony and flying around outside. I tried to keep my voice loud enough for all of them to hear, but it wasn't easy, and it was clear that some of the elders didn't feel comfortable with all this information being public.

Wanting to be careful not to make any enemies of the dragons if I could help it, I did my best to make it sound as if it was no one's fault in particular that no one in the city had known the gate was weakening.

"This is a lot to take in, and we must think about how best to solve the problem. You don't think we have to act so fast as to try and power the gate tomorrow?" the elder who had been kindest to me asked.

"We have more time than that. From what I understood when speaking to Alitas, it has been weakening my whole life and can still hold for now. It will take time to figure out how to power it once more," I replied, hoping to reassure him a little.

"Then, if that is the case, I suggest we adjourn now,

allow the city to process what we all know, and then we will plan your official coronation and make a plan as a group. There is a lot to understand, and we cannot work through it all in one session."

He spoke truthfully enough, and he had a good point.

I backed up to the center of the room.

"Thank you for hearing me and understanding the situation we're in. I look forward to working with you to solve this problem. In the meantime, I would like to rest."

"You will be shown to the royal quarters immediately," he replied, a small smile appearing on his face.

I blinked in shock. I hadn't expected something so fancy. I had been planning to go back to Ben's apartment and offer to share the bed there with my mother.

A guard came forward, eyes shining as he approached me.

"It would be an honor to show Your Majesty the way," he said and motioned for me to go with him.

"I would like my companions to join me," I replied, looking at them. My mother and Ben had already followed me and made it clear they would come too, but Neritas, Flick, Tiffany, and Capricia hadn't moved to join me.

The first three did now, but Capricia took a step back.

"I will return to my duties," she said. "I consider my part in all this done. I escorted Scarlet safely to and from the city and have fought hard to make sure no one was harmed."

"Thank you," I replied, but she didn't look at me, and I wasn't sure that she heard me over the noise of the other elders giving commands and the other dragons talking now the meeting was over.

I had little choice but to follow the new guard.

We moved back out of the chamber, heading in a brand-new direction and to the top of another large tower on the city edge furthest out to sea. Several more dragons bowed and lowered their heads when I walked past. I tried to smile at everyone who met my gaze, not wanting to make any of them feel as if I was lording it over them.

The sheer number who moved out of my way and bowed was far more than I'd expected. It was strange, but it was also a relief.

I was queen, and it had been accepted.

EPILOGUE

Waking up to a breakfast table laden with food after having slept in the largest, most comfy bed I had ever seen had its perks. I grinned as I joined my friends to eat.

After talking about the elders and their reactions the day before, I admonished Neritas for taking the decision out of my hands. He apologized for not warning me and for putting me on the spot, but not for what he'd done, claiming that it was only right that every dragon knew who I was.

Ben had backed him up, and I'd been forced to concede that so far, the city was reacting well enough to the news. But I wasn't entirely sure they were all so thrilled.

Still, for now I was living in the royal tower, and I'd been told that several of the elders were going to come to me to discuss how to handle my coronation and figure out what could be done about the gate and the demons I'd already had to fight.

I was still eating a juicy pear when they arrived, but the elder I liked most smiled when he entered and bowed.

"I hope everything is to your satisfaction," he said when he straightened.

"Yes, thank you," I replied. "Is it you I owe for my feast being so lovely?"

"I had it sent to you, if that's what you mean."

"Then, please, tell me your name so I can know who has all my gratitude."

"I am elder Griffin. At your service. I am one of the few elders who have been running the city long enough to remember serving your father. It is an honor to serve you as his daughter."

"Thank you, Griffin. I hope I can do a good job, but please don't feel you serve me. Hopefully, both of us will serve the city and dragons everywhere. I just want to be able to make the world safe again." I exhaled as I moved over to one of the many comfortable seating areas and offered a seat to him.

Ben and Sienna lingered nearby as I got comfy, but Neritas and Flick stayed at the table, tucking into stacks of pancakes.

"I'm sure that we can make that happen in time." Griffin's face looked tired and almost sad for a moment, a contradiction to the hope his words should have held.

"You don't sound as if you believe what you are saying," I replied, hoping it wasn't too forward of me to call out his incongruence.

"Forgive me, Your Majesty. I am worried that uniting the dragons may be harder than it appears, even with an obvious threat that requires it. Not everyone in the city has reacted well to you claiming the throne. Some dragons like the alternative that having a council of elders has given the city."

I nodded, taking in Griffin's words. Capricia had warned us that not everyone would be willing to accept me, and I'd understood her fears. I had felt them as well. Although I was their queen in title, winning over everyone in unity wasn't going to be so simple.

I thought for a moment and chose my next words as carefully as I could.

"I have a lot to learn, and I won't always get everything right, but if you'll help me, I'd like to try and take care of all the dragons of the world and make them feel heard and seen. Just because the red dragons before me have been known for being hotheads and having difficulties and an arrogant streak, it does not mean I have any."

"That is something I have already learned about you from your teachers and those who know you best. Forgive me, but I had to get an understanding of the dragon who would be giving commands here now." Griffin looked down as if he felt shame over his actions.

I squeezed his hand as my parents did to reassure me without speaking.

"The city is clearly in good hands with you. Thank you. Hearing that you are going to such lengths to be sure makes me feel even more confident that you are someone who can help me. Please tell me if you get a different picture at any point and I don't do a good job of being a good leader."

He smiled and nodded. This was the strangest conversation I'd ever had, but I was pretty sure I'd just appointed my first royal adviser.

"With time, I will see what can be done about those who are whispering, discontented with your claim to rule. In the meantime, I think the best thing to do is to plan a coronation as soon as it can be arranged with sense and tact, and figure out this gate issue along the way." Griffin pulled out a tablet device similar to the one I had, but a little larger and shinier, to show me what the usual procedure for a coronation was.

Once more, I had to pause and process. Within a week or so, I would be crowned queen of the dragons, and whether everyone liked it or not, it was happening. Then I could focus on learning how to channel magic and keep the world's biggest evil locked up. Easy-peasy. What could possibly give me reason for alarm?

THE STORY CONTINUES

The story continues with book four, *Dragon Rising*, available at Amazon.

Claim your copy today!

ACKNOWLEDGMENTS

The third book in each of my series is where I usually feel like I properly settle in and know what I'm doing with the characters and this series was no different. I am glad to feel back on the wagon and enjoying writing as well as reading. Life takes some adventurous turns sometimes and doesn't go the way we would expect. Bryan has been the most unexpected blessing in my life I could hope for. I didn't realize how much things had got out of balance until you came back into my world and helped me see where I had crushed my own dreams and hopes to be accepted by people who only pretended to care. Thank you for being there for me when it mattered most.

To my tiny humans for being as excited as I am about some of the small things and making me feel younger again. I love you both.

To Bear, Andrew, David, Clare and Anne-Mhairi. You are the found family I didn't know I needed this badly.

And a huge thank you to everyone at LMBPN, especially Robin. I am so grateful for everything you do, how enthusiastic you all are and how much you all support me in my author journey. Joining LMBPN was one of the best decisions I ever got to make. My books are in good hands.

Last but not least, to God. You've got this and I'm so relieved.

ABOUT THE AUTHOR

Jess is in the process of changing her name. She's been through a difficult year that leaves her wanting a fresh start and a chance to be the person she's always meant to be. Over the next little while all her books will be moving to Talia Beckett and you'll find all future releases under this author name.

Talia was born in the quaint village of Woodbridge in the UK, has spent some of her childhood in the States and now resides near the beautiful Roman city of Bath. She lives with her two tiny humans (one boy and one girl) and near an amazing group of friends who support her career and life choices.

During her still relatively short life Talia has displayed an innate curiosity for learning new things and has therefore studied many subjects, from maths and the sciences, to history and drama. Talia now works full time as a writer and mummy, incorporating many of the subjects she has an interest in within her plots and characters.

When she's not busy with work and keeping her tiny humans alive she can often be found with friends, playing with miniature characters, dice and pieces of paper covered in funny stats and notes about fictional adventures her figures have been on.

You can find out more about the author and her

upcoming projects by joining her on facebook, by watching her live D&D streams, or emailing her via books@jessmountifield.co.uk. Talia loves hearing from a happy fan so please do get in touch!

Talia is also opening up her discord for fans to come chat about what she's up to, and see a few sneak peaks of future work. There's also a chance to become one of her beta readers. If you'd like to check that out you can do so here.

CONNECT WITH THE AUTHOR

Connect with Talia

Mailing list sign up
Facebook group.
Discord group
Actual play D&D stream: Twitch or Youtube
Email address: contact me here.

BOOKS BY JESS MOUNTIFIELD / TALIA BECKETT

Already published

Urban Fantasy

Dragon of Shadow and Air:

Air Bound

Shadow Sworn

Dragon Souled

Earth Bound

Night Sworn

Dryad Souled

Water Bound

Day Sworn

Pegasus Souled

Fire Bound

Light Sworn

Phoenix Souled

Dragon Apparent:

Dragon Missing

Dragon Seeking

Dragon Revealed

Time of the Dragon (with Andrew Bellingham):

Dragon's Code

Dragon's Inquisition

Dragon's Redemption

Fantasy

Tales of Ethanar:

Wandering to Belong (Tale 1)

Innocent Hearts (Tale 2 & 3)

For Such a Time as This (Tale 4)

A Fire's Sacrifice (Tale 5)

Winter Series:

The Hope of Winter (Tale 6.05)

The Fire of Winter (Tale 6.1)

Guild of the Eternal Flame:

Wayfarer's Sanctuary

Protector's Secret

Healer's Oath

Other Fantasy:

The Initiate (under Holly Lujah)

Writing with Dawn Chapman:

Jessica's Challenge (#5 in the Puatera Online series)

Dahlia's Shadow (#6 in the Puatera Online series)

Lila's Revenge (#7 in the Puatera Online series)

Sci-Fi:

Fringe Colonies:

Alliance

Haven

Rebellion

Rebirth

Reclamation

Star Trail:

Hunted

Sherdan series:

Sherdan's Prophecy

Sherdan's Legacy

Sherdan's Country

Sherdan's Road (A short story in the anthology 'The End of the Road')

The Slave Who'd Never Been Kissed (A short in the charity anthology 'Imaginings')

New Beginnings

Santa's Little Space Pirate

In the multi-author Adamanta series:

Episode 1 – Adamanta

Episode 3 – Excelsior

Episode 8 – Phoenix

Episode 13 – New Contacts

Episode 17 – Sacrifice

Other:

Clues, Claws and Christmas

Non-Fic:

How to Write Lots, and Get Sh*t Done: the Art of Not Being a Flake

Find purchase links here

Coming soon:

Urban Fantasy:

Dragon Apparent:

Dragon Rising

Dragon Defying

Dragon Crowned

Dragon Defending

Time of the Dragon (with Andrew Bellingham):

Dragon's Revolt

Fantasy:

(Tales of Ethanar):

The Pursuit of Winter (#2 in the Winter series, Tale 6.2)

Books under Amelia Price

Mycroft Holmes Adventures:

The Hundred Year Wait

The Unexpected Coincidence

The Invisible Amateur

The Female Charm

The Reluctant Knight

The Ambitious Orphan

The Unconventional Honeymoon Gift

The Family Reunion

The Immortal Problem

The Unremarkable Assistant

Coming soon:

Mycroft 11

OTHER BOOKS FROM LMBPN
PUBLISHING

Sign up for the LMBPN email list to be notified of new releases and special deals!

https://lmbpn.com/email/

For a complete list of books by LMBPN please visit:

https://lmbpn.com/books-by-lmbpn-publishing/

www.ingramcontent.com/pod-product-compliance
Lightning Source LLC
LaVergne TN
LVHW091717070526
838199LV00050B/2436